Sifting

First published in 2015 by
Liberties Press
140 Terenure Road North | Terenure | Dublin 6W
T: +353 (1) 405 5701 | E: info@libertiespress.com | W: libertiespress.com

Trade enquiries to Gill & Macmillan Distribution
Hume Avenue | Park West | Dublin 12
T: +353 (1) 500 9534 | F: +353 (1) 500 9595 | E: sales@gillmacmillan.ie

Distributed in the United Kingdom by
Turnaround Publisher Services
Unit 3 | Olympia Trading Estate | Coburg Road | London N22 6TZ
T: +44 (0) 20 8829 3000 | E: orders@turnaround-uk.com

Distributed in the United States by
Casemate-IPM
22841 Quicksilver Dr | Dulles, VA 20166
T: +1 (703) 661-1586 | F: +1 (703) 661-1547 | E: ipmmail@presswarehouse.com

ISBN: 978-1-909718-40-1
2 4 6 8 10 9 7 5 3 1

A CIP record for this title is available from the British Library.

Cover design by Karen Vaughan – Liberties Press
Internal design by Liberties Press

*The publishers gratefully acknowledge the
financial assistance of the Arts Council.*

Sifting
Uncle Ned &
Other Stories

Mike Mac Domhnaill

Contents

Uncle Ned

You tell and retell until the story is what happened. What *happened* only happened as it happened. The telling is what is and only now, the here and now, this story begins where we wish it to begin. Let's say he looked back at the onion rows and the month is July. He had weeded the onions. Will we deliver sun? Yes, sun. July that year was good. Let the sun stream therefore from the south-east. Morning then? Morning. We'll make it morning for all sorts of reasons. More cheerful. The arc is on the up.

Let us say she is lying there how long. Do we ever know? No. Do we know of happiness? A little. The day before she had gone to the hairdressers. Always cheers a woman up, particularly my mother. Came back with stories. Looking spruced. Beaming. Even with stiffening arthritis. Deforming fingers giving rise to embarrassment. Unable to unlock. But still rolling out the bread. The stiff movement as we walk around the house. God? Throw in his will. Easier to accept. His will may drag us up into the hay barn of happiness. The promise of sweet hay for the long winter.

The latchkey where we left it. Time to give the first call. Mid morning. You open the door and call . . . Call again, can't you. Knock on the bedroom door. Harder for Christ's sake. Harder.

Now open and then . . . Lying there half dressed. As if laid back for rest.

The general kerfuffle and disbelief. Ringing. Doctors. Priests. Relatives. Doctor, Doctor,

something, anything? It's as you see it, I'm afraid. Poor thing, all the pills and medication. She went well.

Why would the sun stream in? Because the house faces south and the sun doesn't care. The venetian blinds let in the bars of sunshine sprinkled through with bedroom dust. The air this morning . . . The air is now choking and the doctor is gone. Having said all that was to be said. The air is choking, the day is choking, the head is gone. The young priest saying we all wish for one more day. Gone.

Soon they arrive. The heavy-set farmer, Uncle

Ned, comes in with one of the younger sons. Was it Jim? 'Oh, well, well. Oh well, well. Poor Kitty to be gone.' And the story then begins. How did it and when and the shock you must have got an awful shock, *shock*, **shock**. My head.

We move to the front room parallel. Equal sun. If sun it is we want. This day. Obligatory. We pour the whiskey. For him. The chair by the window. The fold-up chair obtained in the god-knows-when. Coupons after the war! Never too comfortable, left there in the bay window to gather books, magazines; lazily to accumulate and stack up amid its post-war dreams. The comics. Not all comic. What war but *The* World War, Blitzkrieg from the comics. The good Brits always finally downed the Huns, the bad lads from Germany, swoosh, *Achtung* up your arse, take that, hardly an Irish war; struggles – I'll grant you, troubles, revolts at best, gunmen, killers, troublemakers, sub, what, sub, say it, subversives that's us, those comics came from up the road, across the sea, never bought mind, never – maybe once when sick, *Achtung* and *Gott in Himmel* to save you from the mumps, the measles, and as he settles in . . . the sudden creak and tear and down flops Uncle Ned! The laughing as we pull him up. This day when laughs are scarce. But we imagine her laugh too. The room assumes a new decorum. Sit and reminisce and then the tears. Oh God. Waiting for the arrangements. This is Gethsemane. But they're all *watching one hour with me*, hours becoming minutes and streaming back into hours through some strange egg timer. Once left on my own, time drops in pools, blobs in the lungs, choking for life, control, shivering like a leaf. Grip the door handle. Grip the door handle before emerging. There.

They come and go. In a swirl. 'Ah sure once they died there was no choice she had to take over' – Uncle Ned again. 'Just six weeks between them. She told you about the dog? Howling outside the window. As if he knew. She often talked about that dog.' A soft laugh. 'I don't think he lasted long.'

'Then 'twas all left to her. Oh the baking, the housework, the chickens, the calves – and me landed with the farm. No, no, she was older.

'Oh they were . . . did she say that . . . Ah, the father was hard, ye never knew him, but maybe then he had to be. Different times. Ah well, well. Your mother was that bit wild. She told you about the dance! No, no,' he laughed, 'I was too young for that. Sure I wouldn't take the chance. With *him*? Kit was daft! Out the window of the bedroom. And she was bound to be caught. Sure I told her that. Brought the stick down on her back. It went too far. But that's the way things were and she was al- ways that bit wild. She told ye that herself! Ah, she was a great card.' He trailed off.

'Ah, she was . . . and great to ye when your father

died. Ah sure of course . . . too young. But that's the way. Milking cows, out in all sorts. Ah ye have it soft today. Isn't it true for me, too soft ye have it!' We forced another laugh. A sip of whiskey. 'Well, well!'

Life summarised in these recorded facts. If facts they be. The many gaps. The bits we never know. The lines upon lines of handshakes, my aching back, to the point . . . wishing it to conclude, but yet another, knew her well, cousins in their droves. Flocking in out of the yard, the playing corners, back from other times, so that's where you are now . . .

This story and that.

Oh that? Don't blame me for that! We were all in it. Picking some passage from the Old Testament, or some Epistle, given a choice! And it was only up there reading it from the altar I realised it was for a young death, a young man, and I galloped on through it! I can see her laugh.

The general *ruaille buaille* of arrangements. Hold. Hold on to this branch, hug this tree, feel this earth. Dust back to dust. Preferable, the comfort of the earth than out there in the blue. Best back here. Like the fox. Return. We to follow, so let's cheer up.

What if there is . . . no Well of Love. Love. Love divine, to overcome it all. Here we shuffle at the graveside, mourners coming in their droves. Are they coming out of the ground? Shake hands, shake hands, rattle your brains for a name. Bad at names, what a time to be bad at names. Eavesdrop for a hint. Sorry for your loss.

The comics on that broken chair. The sedate postwar chair. *The Dandy*, Beano gave some fun but then 'twas more grown-up, on to Hotspur with its exploits of goals that shook the net. Roy of the Rovers, hoofing it into the top corner. And the British guns bring down the Huns, in the real wars, not troubles where you see the whites of the eyes, know the neighbours. Not 'troubles' like ours.

'I like to ramble down the old *boreen* . . .'

Now sing 'Mc Namara's Band', sing 'Mc Namara's Band'. Clambering onto your knee, four or five of us, children and cousins, tugging and pulling. The Uncle Ned of old. Great to have an uncle a bit of a rogue. Those times. Now you sit there inside the bay window and we talk to keep the pain at arm's length. 'Ah, she often did. When the hay was in and the milk was dying back, September, she'd be off then with the friends. Off to Lisdoon. They'd cycle all the way. Stop? That now I don't know. She told ye there was always one stop, in Limerick, to break the journey . . . Oh yes, 'twas Lisney's! That was Lisney's eating house.

That's where we all stopped. All the crowd from here.' A soft laugh. 'Ah now, that was a long time back. Cycle it now! Ye would in yere hat! What are you telling me, ye'd need the car to cross the road! Trials of strength? She told ye that. Lifting weights and fellows jumping across the stream outside the spa. Sunday mornings. Who'd jump the farthest. I often saw lads getting soaked. How they weren't killed. Half mad we must have been.' The soft laugh. 'Then cycle home again after the week. Back to the drudgery. Well you might stick to the books! Well, well. Poor Kitty to be gone.'

All the 'no mores'. Edging your vision above the grave. Back with your father and her favourite uncle. Gravestones all around. Beckoning. People gathering in knots. Uneven ground. Bright sunshine, she got that.

'No, it's years . . . Maybe in the loft. You're welcome to it! That old gramophone. She'd say, "We'll put it on, we'll put it on tonight if no one calls." She loved Mc Cormack. Him above them all.'

'A chusla, a chusla, I hear someone calling . . .'

Why don't we play it now for her, you do the winding, nice and even. The old gramophone, needle scratching, endearing. Get Ned to put it on. Perching it there on the table. Brought out for the occasion. There by the fire. Make it an open fire, make it crackle. Now sit back and listen. Leave them to it. We'll back out, gentle on the door handle. Just them. Before any of us. Before dreamt of. No arthritis-aching bones. No dead young husband. No moving into a cold house. The cows are milked. Hear Mc Cormack sing. Hear it out here, from the yard. Let innocence begin.

'Bullets under the mattress! Had she that?' The soft laugh. 'Sure I was hardly born. Maybe now there was . . . I heard they raided a few times. Of course we'd have been burned out. She held it against them after that. Of course our side went with Collins. There wasn't much time for them after that. They'd stay overnight, I often heard. Held it against them for leaving the bullets. Could have been burned out. But it's all in the past. That's where we should leave it. Of course ye had yere rows!' The chuckle. 'Held it against them all her life. Yerra, I remember none of that. Only all the old stories. She was mad for all those old stories . . . And then the Blueshirts!' The soft laugh. 'What was he again – O'Duffy? Sure we were all daft. Yerra, but that soon died off. De Valera, she hated him! Having to kill the calves. Ah, all that's in the past. No wonder ye had rows. But you're as bad, do you know that. You should have more sense. Bullets under the mattress!' The soft laugh.

What if the Tans . . . Mightn't they have planted . . . 'Ara, go away now out o' that! That's a twist your crowd might put on it! Of course we know who did it . . . And most of them only out for what they'd get.' The laugh growing caustic. 'Your mother had it right. Oh mark my words she had. She had indeed.' This time no laugh.

The broken post-war chair, when wars were wars, and not the cheek-by-jowl, the closeness of breath, the dinner quickly set, the moving off at dawn. The broken post-war chair obtained with coupons, standing there aloof, in the bay window, presiding over the delicate window fern. The broken post-war chair. The comics where the English beat the Huns. The 'jolly good!' The 'chin up!' The decent kind of chaps who played it fair and gave the world a decent kind of war.

Then Uncle Ned goes crashing through it all.

Uncle Malachy

Life was flying past
the nineteen-year-old youth.

Re-reading ... Yes ... maybe. Frightening the way time passes. Uncle Mal and Freddy Gibbons here for dinner and chat. The usual. Freddy with the watch:

'Now, Kitty, we'll be leaving at 2:30. Then on to Feenagh. I must have this man back by five.'

His 2:30! The hair coiffed. His Morris Minor, spick and span, kept to itself outside our gate. Talked hurling and football. Hasn't missed an All-Ireland since Noah left the ark.

'Ah but the tickets, Fred, how do you manage that? Every year!'

'Oh, I have my contacts, shall we say, I have my contacts!'

'Of course Freddy here . . .' says Uncle Mal,

smiling, benign, 'Freddy's the epitome of organi-sation! Right Patrick? You're the one in college now. Epitome? Would you say we're right there! Ah yes, Fred is the organised one. Thirty football All-Irelands and what is it? Twenty-nine hurling?'

'God!' I said. 'What year did you start, Fred?'

'Come on now, you're the mathematician in the family, Patrick!'

They can never call me Paddy, these uncles or their straight-laced friends, but I like Uncle Mal, always have.

'Oh . . . 1943? Football! There now, what a record!'

During the dinner we'd get Uncle Mal going on the Provos.

'Do you know what it is, Kitty, I'm going to let the beard grow.'

'What! You're joking, Father Malachy, I can't imagine you with a beard!'

Of course we'd heard this already from the cousins in Dungeeha. Family joke. The bald, round-headed big man of the uncles to have a beard. But it was only imagination. He'd never do it – or get away with it – in the Order.

'Yes, leave it grow and grow with no more of that bother of shaving.' He gazed at the fern on the bay window. 'When classes end I'll be free as I please. I'm going to kick the traces, Kitty! Kick the traces!'

He laughed softly as he went back to his soup.

'Ah, that's great soup, Kitty.'

'Kitty *always* cooks a fine soup. You know that, Mal.'

The crisp tones of Freddy. For everyone else it's always 'Uncle' or 'Father'. Freddy is in the inner circle. Wonder he never joined. Always with priests.

A fine strapping man, our Uncle Mal. Last Christmas when he filled in for the parish priest and was walking up the church in his vestments: 'Oh look!' says Hilda Finnerty, 'It's the moving mountain!' Smirking out over her glasses.

Poor Mother mortified. And of course the same Hilda knew exactly who he was all right. Is there any mercy in this adult world?

We were on to the chicken.

'Ah the stuffing, Kitty. What do you put in it at all! It's the finest.'

'I'm telling you,' says Freddy, 'this woman can *cook*! Sure amn't I always saying it.'

'Oh, go away with yerselves,' – Mother, 'indeed it's only a small offering.'

(I saw Uncle Mal put away one full apple tart once. Slice after slice!

'Kitty, do you know what, that tart is wonderful.'

And off with him with another slice. Mother said he mustn't be fed at all up in the college. But a great worker. His holiday? Back at the home place, Dungeeha, out working in the meadows, digging the garden, anything not to be idle. Our Uncle Mal!)

'Well, what do you think of the North?' This was from Freddy.

Great! Now we're off. There was a pause. Then that timid smile.

'Fred, I must tell ye a great one.' He beamed at the prospect. 'Out in the garden the other day with the students – of course I wasn't meant to hear it. An IRA man arrives at the gates of heaven. Carrying a parcel. Out comes St Peter. "One minute now," says St Peter, "but I'm awfully sorry – *you're* not coming in here." "What do you mean, coming in?" says our man, laying down the parcel. "Ye have five minutes to get out!"'

There was a great chuckle. Of course I had heard it, but coming from Uncle Mal, sure I had to laugh.

'Oh I don't know, Father,' came Mother, 'all very well to be laughing. I gave this poor man a lift the other day coming back from the hospital in Croom – sure I could barely understand him with his northern accent. Whatever he was doing down here . . . He had a drop on him, the poor devil. And he went on and on that it would all come south and we'd have civil war. I wasn't the good of it when he got out at The Cross.'

'You're a terror for giving lifts,' – Freddy. 'You should be more careful, Kitty. An amount of them came down you know, there a few years back when they were burned out. Bombay Street and those places.'

'What a strange name for a street in Belfast – Bombay Street!' – Mother.

'You know the world is changing.' – Freddy – 'I'd watch who I'd be giving lifts to. And I think they're all gone mad up there. Shooting and bombing. Now I like that man, Hume, isn't it? He seems to make a bit of sense. I like him.'

'Ah yes', came Uncle Mal, 'but where did it get him on Bloody Sunday, Fred? All of those poor people . . .' The voice wavering.

There was respectful silence for a while before Uncle Mal broke in again.

'But the British were always the same, wherever they went. Always divide and conquer . . .'

Then he lightened up and there was the moist smile behind his glasses.

'I must tell ye another one I heard from lads in the yard. They *told* me this one, so Kitty, you'll like it! You know the way they talk up there, the accent you find hard to follow . . . Anyway . . . There were three ducks flying over Belfast. There they are, fly-ing along in a row. And the duck at the back says: "Quack!" And then the one in front of him says: "Quack!" And the one in front turns back and snaps: "I can't go any quacker!"'

Again there was general chuckling. Of course I

should have added: Would you say now they were Bombay ducks?

'Well you know,' says Mother, 'when they're there on the television I can't understand half of what they're saying. Now Father Mc Crum, isn't he from up there? I can understand him perfectly when he's around with you.'

'Ah but he's an educated man, Kitty,' says Freddy, 'The bit of education makes the difference.'

'Well now . . .' there was that shy smile on Uncle Malachy's large round face, 'when I'm finished with the teaching – and that's just two years, Kitty . . .'

'You're not retiring, Father Malachy? Sure you're as fit as a fiddle.'

'Oh, I'm afraid I am, Kitty! I'm reaching that age – *tempus fugit*, what! And when I'm a bit freer' – he handled the cutlery as a little distraction – 'I'd like to help out . . . Those lads are out there, just like the flying columns long ago. They're dying on the streets and in the ditches.'

He intertwined his fingers and moving them up and down: 'I could be their chaplain.'

'Oh, Father Malachy! Haven't you enough to be doing down here!' Mother pretending it was her first time hearing it.

'Don't mind him, Kitty,' says Freddy. 'Of course, Malachy, the Tan War left its mark on all of your people down there at the mouth of the Shannon! When we had our own *troubles*.'

'Do you know,' Uncle Mal turns to me, 'that down in Dungeeha we had an open house during the Troubles and into the Civil War? Were you ever shown the trapdoor in the orchard where they were to leave their guns before coming in? Your poor Uncle Pat says he was only half fed growing up with our mother – your grandmother, Patrick – feeding those men on the run!'

'Pat was the youngest, of course,' said Fred. 'I don't know now if Pat has any time for the present crowd though. You should have more sense, Malachy! Keep well away from it is my motto.'

They moved on to the trifle. A nice dollop of cream for Uncle Mal. Fred abstemious.

'Must watch the waist, Kitty, and don't you mind his talk of "out on the hillsides"! It will be all patched up before then. I see that fellow – Faulkner is it? – he'll surely do something with the unionists. He seems a decent enough chap.'

'You know they give nothing until they're forced to.' – Uncle Mal.

'Oh, they can't be all bad, now Malachy. They can't be all bad. Doesn't Father Mc Crum say he had great neighbours growing up and he was in the thick of them?'

'All right until the Twelfth!' said Uncle Mal, 'Then you'd better lie low. All right until the Twelfth!'

'I just wish the killing would stop,' Mother broke

in. 'Didn't we hear enough about it, God knows, and we growing up.'

Freddy saw it was time to change:

'I'm giving Limerick a great chance against Kilkenny.' Back to his favourite tack. 'We have only three weeks you know and with Grimes and Cregan we won't be far off.'

'Don't forget Big Pat Hartigan,' said Uncle Mal. 'He'll be minding the square.'

'And as clean a hurler as you'll find,' rejoined Freddy. 'That's *your* game of course. Fine clean hurling!'

Turning to my mother:

'I'll have to bring this man to a good, tough junior match some evening, Kitty, and we'll show him timber! Ballysteen or Knockaderry! What do you say?'

'If ye may stick to the hurling and don't mind the crowd in the North. That's what I say.

Let them sort it themselves. We had enough of it down here.'

Then Fred is out with the watch. The time, the time!

When we moved outside it was again that pleasant afternoon sun presiding over these mid-August days. Uncle Malachy manoeuvred his large frame into the pristine Morris Minor. Mother joked after they left that you could see the car sink down when he sat in.

'Fred is so proud of that car.' And, turning to me: 'I hope the springs don't give!'

Diary: 14 March 1975

Hoping for happiness that might befall. Hoping for happiness . . .

Looking at the picture taken at the Olympic . . . Yes . . . *that might befall* . . . Arm around her shoulder; coy with her hands on her knee, her thumb keeping down the miniskirt. *Hoping for happiness . . .* what to make of it all?

Reading back through the diary and that day in the sitting room. And now Uncle Mal to be gone. Died in his sleep. Way to go! says the Yank. Poor Uncle Mal.

Mother is very upset. Ever since Dad she has relied on our Uncle Mal. Himself and, I suppose, Uncle Pat. At Christmas always a turkey. And it too big for the oven! And the odd bag of potatoes. The Order seeming to allow these acts of kindness to his sister-in-law.

'A wonder,' Aunt Molly would say, 'a wonder they might give to a widow.'

Died in his sleep. There in the college. Not in a barn in Tyrone or a ditch near Aughnacloy!

He died with it still going on, poor man. How it always affected him. Big and kind. Never once saw him cross. Maybe the pupils . . .

The night we gave that group a lift to the dance. Driving back from Grange. Didn't know who we were. One of them, a student of his, pipes up:

'Father Mal? Of course, a slave driver! A pure slave driver!' was his verdict. 'If there's no work in the garden he's out with us pulling ivy off the walls. Dead set against ivy! Oh, a pure slave driver!'

A great laugh in the back of the car. Then an awkward silence.

'Now you wouldn't be . . . ? Oh God, now we're landed!'

DIARY: 16 MARCH 1975

> *I know that breaking*
> *from the chains that bind*
> *must have meant . . .*

Everything happened inside the grounds. The funeral Mass with the few anecdotes of the man they called Father Mal. Light-hearted enough. *Must have meant . . . must have meant a kind of freedom.* Maybe they feel they have a guaranteed ticket – like Freddy! All his life there teaching how to sow and reap. Prayer. For them, he had done his bit. He was *theirs*. And he was buried in *their* plot. Their worker come to rest.

'A wonder we got the cup of tea itself.' – Aunt Molly. Always sharp.

'And they inside with their four-course meal.

Full of their old guff.'

Always resenting the top brass, with their days out at the cattle shows. Their pictures stuck up in the paper.

'And no beard, Mam, you're spared all that! And no running round with the Flying Column!'

'Oh, the poor man never meant it I'm sure . . . Just some cracked talk when Freddy brought him out in the car . . . Just some cracked talk.'

Writing for Joan

Trapped in a chair. No locks or shackles. Despair. Just despair, at the News. The never-ending News and the sister tearing up her mortgage papers in front of everyone last night. Whiskey-fuelled.

Like I'm floating. Like we're all floating.

What will I do today? To the window! I am sitting inside this window which sometimes reflects a shadow, sometimes it's the shrub, rounded by my mother – the fights we have, I want it left to grow its own way, reach its fingers outwards, to sun and space, but no, she's out again to round it off. Looks neat, she says, when clipped. And sometimes it's a bird, picking on the stale crumbs.

If I don't finish this I'll go mad. I can't turn up without some feckin' thing written down. She said they might stop the dole. I'll tell her to stick it . . . I can't get out of this chair. Get back onto Facebook? No. No. I'll have to start this. Start it before finishing it, now there's a good idea. And my sister heading off. 'Fuck the land of our fathers,' says she, 'and fuck the whole bloody island.' Then Dinny the Literate goes on about some sow devouring her own. 'This fuckin' sow is just pushing us out into the shit.' The easing down when Mother restored some calm.

'Now, now there's always a way back—'

'A way back! They shoved the money at us. Shoved it.'

'There's more than you in it—'

'Oh big deal so I'm not alone, more than me. Hallelujah!'

Then we all started singing like Cohen, some like Jeff Buckley, others like crows like me:

'Broke your throne and cut your hair.'

Until we howled out:

'It's a cold and it's a broken Hallelujah!'

What a crescendo! There in the kitchen. Hallelujah! Blasted it out for the neighbours. 'Shss, shss!' from Mother. 'Ye'd wake the dead.'

Dinny the Literate and the sow with her litter – oh, what whiskey can do! Write it down, they said, before you forget it. Whatshername will love it.

The window. The window has got rid of the sun and now I can see my face, shadow. Will it tell us our age? Will this be my story for her? She'll say I stole it. She has her job to do – Mother. Oh Mother will you just give over. I'll give her: My face at the window reflects my emotions. It is dull, it is grey, it is mercilessly thin, it is the face of a spectre! Since the mickey-mouse job in the bank went, this is me. Floating there in that pane of glass. And me trans-fixed in this chair. A pain in the arse this chair. No birds today. No crumbs so no surprise there. Any worms? Not a worm for the blackbird. The cheeky robin. I only ever liked wrens. Will I give her a story on my life with the wrens!

There in the little rounded nest peeping out are twenty little wrens. Each smaller than the other. Oh yes they have lots of eggs. Most sure to get caught, one way or another. Like my thoughts. If I have enough thoughts today will one survive and fly? If I apply for one more job – before I blow my bloody mind – if I apply for one more job will that be the one to fly? Now we're motorin'.

And the wren – I'm getting a run on this one – flies the highest in the end. Remember the second-year book and that mad English and history teacher, your man with all the hair. How did he ever eat his yogurt . . . through all that hair!

> The wren it seems is a canny bird
> and hangs out with the eagle
> but when the eagle soars on high
> the wren pops up and beats him!

Maybe that wasn't it but something like it. And

Fogsy thought it was great. I should have liked that teacher because he was daft, like me. Only I'm daft sensible. To get in the door for a job I'll have to look the part, won't I. No beards, hate them anyway. He allowed us to write ''em' instead of 'them' and stuff like that. He was great, looking back.

Oh the wren she is a canny bird! So now Joan! (She likes us to call her Joan. What else would we call her? Miss? At this stage of the game! Isn't she wonderful letting us call her Joan.)

This chair that I'm stuck to . . . Made by my father's uncle – your grand-uncle, she'll say. That'll make her feel clever. My father's uncle fashioned this chair out of ash from the hedge beyond. My father, it seems, was very proud of that. Fashioned out of the hedge beyond! But then he fashioned his exit and left me, Ma and Sis all to ourselves. Like it was a little gift. To just . . . be gone.

So proud of that chair – Ma – and it to be fashioned out of the ash beyond. Well Joan, where were we? The wren. I too will attach myself to some soaring eagle and bounce higher and say: F-you! Now who's higher? I'll lay so many eggs one's bound to hatch a winner. And then we're saved. Ma can stop fashioning that round ball of a bush, can get in a gardener. Might have more taste. Might even have a wren's nest in it to round off our little scéal. Will Joan go for that, or will she say, try again. Like last week she said it was not one bit sincere! If we're to make any progress you will have to record your feelings.

That is why I am here. To help.

Why didn't she give us a list of questions. Ones you could tick. Will I look at Facebook? No . . . No. What else could I give her? Take the eagle's point of view? No. Enough birds. That blank backyard. And that roundy bush. This bloody chair fashioned from the ash. And *súgán* cords that wear into your arse! The father admired the *súgán*. And then he was off.

Gone. Vaporised, you might say.

So if not the wren or the eagle what then? The sparrow, Edith Piaf. Why am I sticking to the father's stuff? Left all those Piaf records. 'Ah, Little Sparrow,' he'd say, 'none to top her!' Now I download the stuff. Not bad. If I give her the father's story? No . . . No. There's no start or finish there. A middle, yes. But you need all three, she says. A start, a middle and an end. What a load of cobblers. Looking out that window there is only blank. No start, middle or end.

Will I give her Sis? Too close to the bone. Too raw. The way she exploded last night. Herself and Tim off to God knows where. Australia. Off to dig up Ned Kelly's bones. Put on his tin canister. Bushranger. Get the hell out of here at all costs. Hate the place, hate the place, look where it's left us, look where it's left us. Hate it hate it. That's Sis.

And I'm stuck in the chair. There's Ma now for the tea and still nothing penned to the page. Now that has a ring to it: Nothing penned to the page. Even though it's a laptop. She would surely take the bait. Even old Fogsy would have liked that. 'Good for a fifteen-year-old,' he'd say. 'You should keep it up.' Yogurt. I can't think of him without the yogurt. Wasn't it Molyneaux saw him eating in the teachers' staffroom. Sent in for copies. There was Fogsy, mouth wide, eyes to heaven, about to drop in the spoon of dollop. With the shock of Molyneaux bounding in without even a knock, plopped on the beard! Cursed and swore. Then gathered himself and spluttered: 'Did you ever hear of knocking or can you read? *Múinteoirí Amháin*. Swahili to you? Or have you recently joined us? Recently qualified, Molyneaux? Hum?'

And he rattled on, says Molyneaux, about American universities and it wouldn't surprise him if they didn't have a degree in surprising teachers. Write away for it! So that soon he was laughing at the idea. 'You may now,' says he, 'remove those copies. Careful now, Molyneaux, they may contain some hidden gems! Ho-hum!' Molyneaux was forever telling it.

The *súgán*. He had another one about the *súgán*, old Fogsy. Some old Irish story or other. The way he'd tell it like it was happening there in front of you. Eyes and beard going with him acting the parts. Some of us in stitches, more with their eyes to heaven.

'Excuse me, sir, is this on the course?' Lafferty, the points chaser. Pity Fogsy didn't hit him. Was it the father or the daughter? Anyway it doesn't matter. They wanted rid of him, this fellow who was after the daughter. And they thought up the trick with the hay. Keep winding. *Casadh an tSúgáin* – that was it. Turning and turning making this hay rope and all the while backing him towards the door. He – mesmerised, I suppose – until he was out in the yard winding, winding and . . . Bang! Closed the door and my poor maneen was out in the cold.

There Joan. How to get rid of people in good old Ireland!

This chair. When they fashioned this chair did my father wind the *súgán*? Must have to say he was so proud of it. And now what would he think of poor Sis heading off with her effing and blinding the whole shagging lot. And glad to leave it behind. Never mind that auld rot of wanting to return to Paddy's Green Shamrock Shore. Bloody come-all-yees. Hate it hate it never again want to see it.

But I'm stuck to this chair with the window, the bush – Joan what do you want? My whole bloody life on a plate? The start the middle the end. Be honest. In this haze? Be honest. There's the ash and twisted hay that keep me off the floor. There's the shock when the sun goes in and I only see the spectre. Fogsy's stories of the Famine and fearful figures. About to topple into oblivion. The grass around the mouth. No music then . . . But then he'd get excited. There was music in *some* quarters. Where they still ate well and didn't venture abroad from the homestead for fear of what they'd see. Maybe the birds stopped singing, like Auschwitz – ye've heard of Auschwitz? – oh God, is there anything within these walls?

No stories from the Famine, Joan, to lighten up the road.

No birds singing so all my bird stories are for nothing. But hold on, Joan, there's the ones he drew on the board. The Irish having lost or drawn. Or should have won. The Wild Geese with their long necks straining into the breeze. Heading off for the French battle fields. Will that do us Joan? Wild Geese, with me stuck here to the chair. And Mother calling me now for the tea. Telling Sis God is good and it will all work out like she's read the script. Fashioned from some hedge beyond. She's learned to accept, our mam.

There's always the phone and you'll be better off. She's sending poor Sis from the nest, that's it

Joan, will we wrap it up like that though from my window there's no birds at all today.

As I sit in a chair which reminds me of Dad – I never got to call him Da. The chair that Mother always admires. Fashioned as it was . . . from the hedge beyond . . . while I listen to Edith Piaf.

You Give Witness

You give witness, by the lapels, lifting off the ground comic-wise, unreal strength, must be mad that kind of energy, unreal shall we say – you shall not, you shall not – this is all too real as you will see. You give witness, eyes bulging, opposite the church, where else, The Metaphor Chase, my idea already nobbled. You give witness, the eyes inches from mine. Knew your father, ah a nice quiet man, can I touch you for a quid, the sting, always a sting in the tail, so much for the palaver about my father, the few bob, bottom line, half the town driven mad looking for the next metaphor, now see what you've started, never think things through do you, all very fine coming up with these ideas, all hunky-dory, and then the outcome, never thought through, no prize you said, you mean it's for fun, man, for fun, oh yes, oh yes, tell them what they want to hear, impossible to decipher, words to that effect. Oh who am I to put words in your mouth with your confusing rigmarole

Dipping into pocket, feel around, must keep the price of the dance, his beseeching face, there's all I have, a decent lie, he knows, I know, knew my father, could have been anyone, nice quiet man, covers a multitude, nice to hear all the same when some spoke of alcohol, falling off the bike on his way home, maybe too given . . . Oh dear. Pull up the blankets so's not to hear

What were they thinking asking me to come up with the clues? With a month to go to Christmas, a seasonal search we might call it. '74 All Over, an ominous title, joint decision. The final joint decision. Now over to you. A list of metaphors, within a mile radius, say, of the church. No bother. 'Sheep on High' depends a bit on the forecast, that kind of weather, send them up to the sky, one joint each before they set off, nothing too way out, they said, we can handle it, count the leaves on the beech tree – that means I have to count, take a branch and multiply same by, say one hundred and forty. Never prove me wrong. Allow for wind, attrition of the elements, and half of them won't know a beech tree from Adam. Do they know Adam? *That* you might say, is the . . . conundrum. Chestnuts . . . pot smokers are more into dreamy chestnuts, lounging about reading *Siddhartha* under the enclosing horny branches. It evokes, doesn't it?

There to be a tavern nearby. Fill it in. Don't spare the palette

Knew him well, poor man, too early to die, but that same, well-remembered, nice quiet man, is that all you have, well thanks all the same, make a hero of my father will you and I'll dig out the price of the dance, be off home with myself, half happy, swap you my alcohol haze for your memories, touched up with his kindness, his understanding, his general conviviality. Or not, as you wish, for you to play with the memory sticks. Control, Alt, Delete. Now you've swirled up from the seventies to present day, present day that was, that is. A fine man, you'll say, knew him well, ah sure died too young. Any chance of a few bob, in any time frame, give it to me now even that I'm dead this twenty years, we'll dance in the graveyard. No, your good father's not in here, would be sacrilege, this corner's for us vagabonds. Give us a quid

They're making off down South Quay, 'Goat Street' you prefer, same here, the old name, before the poshness set in, 'Would You Put a Paper Ship to Sail?', maybe at best, there're some of them clambering over the rocks where once washed the washerwomen, steps and all, organised must have been, the Normans, though they relaxed into our company, took a while, some of them scamper over the rocks, the crossing stones, stepping stones from Norman to Gael, now that was easy, to 'Daft Man's Castle', Fuller's Folly, has to be, they've got that too the bright ones, they mustn't have inhaled, they shall inherit the earth or at least the business end, acumen that's what they have but see them get to the clouds, there's the rub, abide with me here outside the church

Ah you'd see him in Lynch's or behind at Kennelly's, nice quiet man, but given at times to pranks, there's no pranks now, them times it was all pranks, that's all you have, well that same, when Old Kennelly was out for the day, came back to his well-run public house to find your father stretched with bottles scattered round, himself and a few of the pals, oh characters, a right bunch, out for the count *mar dhea*, when anyway in comes Old Kennelly, ah you never knew him, but a strict oul fella mind you and of course – flabbergasted, What's this! What's this! They left him stew for a while and then up they shot in fits! Caught you out again, Tomeen! That was the kind of man. Innocent times, innocent times, and that's all you have, well that same

Climbing the walls they are, storming the ramparts, a bit dangerous this, not in the script, some of them could fly by the looks, 'He Wrote in Lingos

Three', has to be the bauld Gearóid Iarla our much prized poet of Norman stock, settled in like the best and applied his quill to Gaelic verse, as well as the others, educated men in those times, but then he was off to Lough Gur to ride around the lake wearing out his horse's shoes, whatever he did to deserve, no grave here to visit, here in our beloved. Out of sight now bar the shouts and shrills as they vie for his writing desk, now where's it hidden, where else but the dungeon, they'll be a while

Another time they went to all this trouble scooping out the turnips for the candles and waiting then behind the Home for old Kit Mc Guire, known to stay out till all hours, anything for the laugh, and wait they did, out by the paupers' graves, is it Bóithrín na Plá that narrow lane, must have been frozen by the time she came, with their sheets draped and ready for a bit of caterwauling but all they got was: Good night, good sirs, an' if ye're dead God rest yere souls an' if ye're alive 'tis a quare hour of the night ye're out! And off with her, cool as a breeze, into Dungeeha. So much for that, And that's all you have, well that same, ah a bit of a lad you might say, but a nice quiet man, up for the lark was all

'The Golden Apples of the Sun' will bring them to the doctor's orchard, where we sported and played and rawked apples in the autumn, and then I'll string them through the demesne, 'At Swim Two Bucks', will bring them to Mc Cann's Pool, the poor man's Ballybunion, where we dipped. 'Poorer and Poorer' will bring them back around to Maiden Street where the boast is 'None Were So Poor' and anyone from up the road is only a pretender. While the Coole off our street was the poorest of all. When they're not at *Siddhartha*, they're into love man peace and brotherhood, how long will that last, but a few have sidetracked onto Flann O' B so they'll enjoy the above, I'll have some friends left when it's all done, but the sky, the sky's the limit, or is it, where does it start and finish, there's one for when they're coming down: 'What is the Stars, Joxer?'

Went for a shoot of course, loved that, heading out around Monagea and places, now did he bring back much, that's another matter, but he loved the shoot. Tracey and himself off with their dogs, nosing about in the wilds trying to rise a bird, a pheasant, even the woodcock. But what they ever brought back, now that's another matter – not much if you ask me. Cleary was the man to bag them and then the gibing there'd be, back in Kennelly's, the slaggin' they'd have and that's all you have, well that same, a lovely man

Yes, we've led them a merry dance, now they're skittering on the Iron Bridge, 'An Droichead Iarainn' to test their rusty Gaelic, while some are legging it up the Mass Path, 'The Way of Truth', what devils of clues, whatever it was now wearing off they appear a touch down in the mouth, no longer an option to ascend to heaven or wherever it is the clouds traverse, the blue beyond, the grey more often, the 'Sheep on High' leading them to no Cloud Nine but to shepherds' curses and I'd better be away as they gather forces, off out the Cork Road helter-skelter, nudge in here with me and not a word mind, not a word until the tally-ho dies, what's this here in the hedge but the band-wheel cross made up at which forge we can only surmise, quiet now, here in the hedge sit back, in memory of this poor Dwyer *chap* (that's how he's called in the last dispatch!) while above in Churchtown not a mile away his brother too laid low, amazing we say that only two outsiders killed, be they Regular or Irregular (imagine being called an 'Irregular', what names – whisht!), the West Limerick crowd they say shot in the air but these two took it full on, Eddie and Denis, and here we are lying, for God's sake hush, they'll tear me apart for the final hint, too bookish by far, while their sense of humour was good at the start it's always the way when the competition starts, even the love brigade start to carp, and hungry then from checking castle and glen, getting doused crossing the Arra, and all for this cul-de-sac, hush will you here by Dwyer's Cross, and the other in Churchtown where his

brother, poor man, tried to stop the Free Staters'
eighteen-pounder from landing its shells in the
Castle Yard, where Irregulars (imagine – whisht!)
lorded whatever was left, hush will you, they're
moving by, beating the bushes

And then of course he had to cycle the seven miles
to work in all kinds of weather, rain hail or shine
couldn't be good for his weak chest – oh don't you
mind that priest with a drink that day at the wedding saying he was a weak little man, you should
have hit him! But no, he hardly meant any harm,
and you know he was smaller than the rest, the rest
of his clan, ah yes, and the asthma caused him to
cough that bit, poor man, and is that all you have,
well that same. Your father was a generous man,
now I'll say that, as decent a man as ever I met. Fid-
dling around in my pocket, here take that, forget
the dance, the country-and-western band. Oh now
a fine man he was, your father

'Run with the Hounds' an easy one thrown in, so
they don't give up, think they're back in the game
searching the Coursing Stand for clue number
seven, not pretty out the back with the briars and
bottles but that's where they're gone. The ha-ha
was for the erudite, the Castle Demesne know-it-
all, 'You'll Laugh When You Land' was all I gave.
At least they're off my scent, the humour wearing

off. Lynched I could be, lynched. All started at the table quiz, and now I have them whizzing around. Like headless chickens on too much dope. The lime kiln and the brother O'Dwyer, we'll bring them to the other spot: 'He Stood in the *Bearna Bhaoil*'. The Gap of Danger. Say a prayer – they've nothing left that lot. Read then from the Upanishads! While I cower here on the Cork Road beside this poor O'Dwyer's ghost. Wait until the tally-ho dies – that's where . . . that's where we'll rendezvous, 'Repair to Horse and Hound', maybe a live guitar twanging out a nasal Dylan yarn in our Tally-Ho Tavern while they drift on up to nirvana. Quizmaster supreme stretched supine, I'll be ferried home in the dead of night. Have we picked out a waning harvest moon

The shirt off his back – that's what he'd give, the very shirt. No dance tonight with this much change. Only to dream a skewed dream by the Arra, no – we dream by the dark-flowing Daar. 'The Bridge on the River that Rhymes with a Dragged-out War' – that one I didn't give. Too much, man, they'd say, too much.

Felix

I am walking back to the flat after . . . It is about nine, nine-ish. It must be September, October. (Leaves were crackling underfoot. Can we put a year? Maybe 1982. Thereabouts.)

I'm sure they are behind me. Scoffing. I can hear it. I walk fast but they keep up with me. Christ! There's no one else on the street. By the high wall of the training college. On the other side neat gardens placid in front of old dark-plaster houses. Faster I walk and they're still with me. Consolation: I have only a few pounds on me. *The pay cheque*? No, no, at home. Left it in the wardrobe after supper.

I am running now. Like bloody hell. Never get to the junction. Am I that slow a runner? They've just lengthened their strides, getting to me, marching, sort of.

Big fellow. God, he's taller than me. Young fresh face. Smiling maliciously. Up beside me now.

Close-cropped fair hair. Barrel chest. Small fellows, ugly, with knives: preferable. This one positively attractive. (That is your cue. You now know. Who. What. Your opinion is formed. Laugh if you will.)

And now I am running desperately. There is sweat trickling into my eyes. Clammy under my coat. Wish I didn't have the coat, could go faster. But, I am racing. They just walk faster to keep up.

The big fellow strides beside me, smiling menacingly across at my terrified face. They are all enjoying the hunt. That's all they want. Not money. That will come later. Enjoy it.

As long as I escape mutilation. A flash before my eyes. Was it a knock on my head from behind? The sniggers.

Standing like a scarecrow. That's how it will end. Tattered clothes. Pockets out-turned. Hands out-turned. Blood. Probably trickles from nose and teeth. And tears.

But it will not be the end. I will get home. I will *live*.

I stall in desperation. Quite out of running. Getting no nearer the junction. The junction where there would be witnesses. Maybe better without witnesses. They enjoy an audience.

Fairy! Fairy! A soft chant. I stall. The tall one has changed. Now he's Twohig. Oh, relief. And back along I see them. The last, the small fellow, is Clancy. Clancy talks.

How's Felix!
And there's a laugh.

I wake up beside M—. I cannot mention names, you understand. A small town, even though they call it a city. And this is grimy business, you will, most of you, will feel. Call him Mole.

Yes, I'm a man. The story so far is by a man. That puts you at ease, I hope. A dream? Of course. It's better than the other one. It must have been the Vietnam study I did. Contemporary America was my thesis. Now to some of you I'm boasting. But we generally are, aren't we? Intelligent. Arty. Arty-farty, you probably laugh. Yes.

Being thrown out of a helicopter. You know what the Yanks did over the jungle. *Ve haf vays off making you tok!* one would mimic. No, not Spike Milligan, The real thing.

And they'd whoosh him nearer the exit. Swirling. Thousands of feet above. Not too low. *Zeese yellow bastards could surfife on trees, no? Haw, haw, haw!*

But they rarely talked, those obstinate little yellow men. Gibberish. Or a stony reticence. Some didn't even seem to mind. Not until the last instant, that is. Then shriek. Boot the yellow bugger.

But some nights I am over the hatch. And the brown mass of jungle swirls beneath. And canyons. Oh jeez . . . And Clancy is always there. The only friend I had, most of the time. Ran with the hare. But slipped over to the hounds always before the kill. Especially in the last years. It must have become obvious. And he had to cover for himself. Now I understand. But then I didn't. Naturally. Not when you're in the thick of it.

Clancy my friend. Clancy my friend. I'd not sleep thinking of the betrayal. And worried sick about myself. One summer I got a girlfriend. A friend was all she wanted, Marie.

Made sure I got the word around. Through Clancy. I think it helped in that year. Or maybe they just got tired. Looking back, I'd say fourteen to sixteen was the worst.

I think it was from a television programme they got it. You know with nicknames. Like good jokes. Never quite sure where they started. But Felix stuck. I still react to it.

It even came home from boarding school with me. A few fellows from round about brought it back. You all loved it. The fun of it. Soon only in the home, the less and less comforting home, was I called Jack. My older brother? I never found out how he felt. He was a great mixer. Not as good at school as me. Anyway, I was the favourite. So Bill took off with a few of the lads and has been in America for years.

Yes. Once. Two years ago. I stayed with him only a day or two though. Then took in LA and San Fran.

'I'm doing a thesis on contemporary America.'
'Well get a load of that! No shit!'

His wife was a bit more interested but I didn't want to embarrass him by staying around.

Often have arguments with my colleagues – I enjoy my work – about the States. After the way I took them apart on Vietnam. Now Nicaragua, they say. Etc. Etc. Even Mole here argues. But I developed a love for the place. Things were free, carefree, for my type in the big cities.

I have to convince himself here that it's not so bad. Then I'm off.

Consolation? Well, the famous actors. Everybody knows about them. Lived together for years. But did they . . . do you think . . . ? Love to know, wouldn't you? And how . . . ? Yes, you're a sordid enough lot. Well, up yours!

Toughened, haven't I? There was the case of the actors, like I said. Everyone just *had* to admire them. So they were caught. Found out too late. So they didn't all speak with a high-pitched lisp.

'Shucks,' as one corporal used always say as the little yellow being plummeted, faint scream . . . to his death.

You don't always know, do you? That's the worst part for you. Take Mole here, the sleeping hunk beside me. Snores. And talks . . . Doesn't dress 'snazzy'. Remember the word? Of course. Especially you,

Clancy. You were always using it. You had a great nasal twang to it. Would always bring a guffaw.

The rest of you. Names? Doesn't matter. Mine didn't matter to you.

Felix, Felix, the cat Felix.
Prowls all night looking for dicks.

Which of you made that up? Not much, poor rhyme, but it always got a laugh. Written on my desk in the final year. When the gibes were dying off. Subtlety creeping in, God help us!

Yes. My English compositions. You loved to hear those read out. You could always down a swot. But the English comp! You had to admire. The few acquaintances . . . the few I had in the last year, were got on the strength of those. Fellows with a slight literary bent. Not friends, mind you. They wouldn't risk that.

I slept a bit more peacefully though, that last year. My star was beginning to rise. I could see yours fixed. The jobs you'd get. The settling down. Match talk. Pint talk. Woman talk.

Woman friends? Of course I have. Admirers of my flamboyance, I'd say. Perhaps that's a boast. You think? I have no shortage of company.

I know you wish to know about Mole. What a name I've chosen for him while talking to you! Little figures from the past, I am pushing you one by one out the little hole. Watching you swirl. Saying, 'Shucks'!

Of course I'm only joking. You, I've forgiven. But I wish you wouldn't follow me in my sleep. Tonight, for instance, I am here lying in sweaty sheets. *You've recalled the clammy boyhood of a tortured youth* – that's more like it. The style of my compositions.

But I'm not up to flowery stuff tonight. I'll have to change or I'll catch my death. I'm getting cold, sitting up here addressing you lot.

Mole? A great hunk of a fellow! You've warmed to me, I can tell. It was that mention of the compositions. But I won't embarrass you with my feelings. If I returned to that flowery prose God knows where it would stop.

He's my type. We get on well. Roles? Him, her? Of course. I'm 'her'. You guessed that. You've reverted to the sniggering bunch again. Come on schoolboys, snap out of it!

We don't actually live together. Just meet from time to time. That way it's not too dependent. And my research keeps me busy. I don't think – I'm only guessing, mind – I use up as much sexual energy as the average married man. Now I could be wrong. So I have more drive for my work, my research. The actors I mentioned. All that energy into acting. Well, it's a theory. And the mix of passions. Adds life. Flamboyance – I think *that's* the word.

Pity for you? No, I wasn't being offensive. To me you *died* at eighteen. Round about then. Were sighted only on the periphery. Overestimate myself? Well maybe I do. That is for you to judge.

Once I used to wish you'd all have sons who would turn out like me. Force you into torment. Force you to confront. But that is no longer my wish. I no longer care one way or the other.

America . . . Yes, I'd like to go there for a few years. I have the qualifications. Mole here, well he'd get on well, out there, I think. But he's happy as he is. I really criticise him fiercely at times, for leading such a double life. Rubs it off. Not as sensitive as me.

But he's great . . . Sorry, I promised. Not to embarrass.

Now please depart and let me alone in my sleep. No more threats. No walking beside me, sniggering, while I race.

Clancy . . . you weren't the worst of them. Of course I forgive you. You had to survive too. Butty, they called you . . .

We were two weak links in a strong boyish chain, not destined to survive side by side. That last composition-style was for you!

At last we can laugh.

The Chalice

I'm here in the Workhouse. Over here in this row. I SAID I'M HERE IN THE WORKHOUSE. Over here in this row. We're over the Laundry. *Can't you hear them*, down below?

Well then. Come closer, I'm not as I was. The man who found the chalice. Me. It was me. 'I,' says her ladyship, Lady Godiva! On one of her visits. Another one of ye! One of the Guardians. Themselves and their Poor Laws. I found it and of course Jimeen claimed it. Mrs Quin did all right out of it and His Lordship, Bishop You-Know-Who, did right well out of it. Nuns' property really so in the sight of the Almighty he's away in a hack, no problem spinning it out to St Peter above at the Pearly Gates. Nuns' property, Church property, ergo – my property! Ergo – you laugh, but you don't go to Mass, if you did you'd hear lots of that.

Where was I? Oh, yes. As the man said, it wouldn't take a Jesuit.

I pulled out. Of course I did, what with Jimeen and his mother claiming the hoard, but it was my spade, there in the fort, that tipped the stone, and, says I, 'That's a hollow sound,' and bent down to investigate, neat as you please, the chalice and the pins, snug in their little nest.

I'm here in the workhouse, heading for the Paupers' Grave. I SAID I'M HERE IN . . . Shhh! Will I whisht? They'll call for the Master. But sure I'm nearly spent. Little the same man can do now. There's arguments about who got what but I'll tell you as sure as I'm here in this bed that I got naught. Or little enough, compared . . .

You'd like to see the wheel, the Workhouse Wheel? Come on and I'll show you. Let me get hold of your elbow. Your auld schoolmaster used to talk about it . . . There. Round and round they'd walk, pushing before them, grinding the corn. That's the wheel. Often left to the women! You'll need to give that a big 'W' – are you writing it down? God bless your pen.

Yes, yes. That's the Stone-breakers' Yard. You want to try your hand at that? Ah-ha!

You're here . . . you're here wondering have I any more to tell. How was it coming in? When you're poor you'll do anything. And bitter, bitter I will admit. I'd only have drank it, that's what was said. Maybe they're right.

The day came nice and bright and myself and

Jimeen approached the ring fort to start forking out the prawteens, no sign of blight.

Approaching the gates no one wants to approach, those gates with their high surrounding walls. Too high to see in, too high to see out. My father had worked on the stone, imagine that! Look up on your way out and maybe one of those is one that he cut – a mason by trade, something I never got. That passed on to my brother Matt. For me the spade and the *spailpín* work. Be sure to look up, on your way out.

Come on while there's a bit of a *sos* and see if you can push the Wheel. That's how 'twould be. All day long. The novelty'd soon wear off. Left to the women half the time, but you know all about that – the poor Master under the cosh when the Guardians found it out. A great hullabaloo. Oh, we know more than you think! You'll walk me back.

Over you go then, to poor old Jack. Sure I worked for him too – when he was well off. Too fond of the drop. Like many the one.

That didn't take you long. Oh? He tells that to one and all! 'Look down my throat.' He'll open up with his finger pointing down. 'Take a good look.' And he'll wait while you take a gawk. 'There's three farms of land gone down that gullet!' Over and over, poor man.

September. We set off for the *ráth*, the old fort in towards the village, where we'd planted that year. There's some that wouldn't go near – you know – the fort, the *ráth*, Reerasta! That's what it's called, you have it right. What it means? Sure that I can't tell. Little time we had for all that. That went to the grave with those gone before. But the bauld Mrs Quin said as long as you don't touch the ring of *sceachs* we'll be right as rain, and do you know what, they were the finest of spuds to be dug that year.

Do you hear me speak from this bed? Will I shss? I'm settled again. Settled.

★

I'll take the high road and you'll take the low road. Again the rattle of the stick. In the porch. The black of night. Mam shushing us. 'Whisht will ye? Quiet for God's sake.' Inclined to laugh. Inclined to be afraid. But we had Mam. *I'll take the high*, settling down. Then a rattle of the stick again. Against the door. A grumbling of curses. *Mallachtaí ón tseanshaol.*

Three small children and their mother. In the one bedroom. Recently widowed. She is your mother but she is way younger than you are now. You can sense the fear but you snuggle close and, somehow, are not afraid. You are five and have seen the gate, the walls, the little entry house where Mary Jane rules the coming and going of these men of the road. Strictly closed at six o'clock. The overflow in sheds, hay barns, or in our front porch. Singing drunk. The Bonny Bonny Banks of Loch Lomond. The Workhouse is now the County Home. Ireland is free. Do you hear me? IRELAND IS FREE! Cool down.

★

Oh the Master often comes round. He does. He's not the worst. The smell at times. When there's fever. However he stands it. And I think of my cup, my chalice and pins, under that stone in September.

When all else fails, welcome haws! And there were haws that year, tons of them ripening that September. Blackberries too. Poking out of the hedges, a few there ready for picking. I can still almost reach with my fingertips.

My father? Oh the father, Matty, he seldom or ever spoke of it. What you're now calling the Famine. Nor did he have a year for it. His brother died in here. After the father helping to build it! You'll look at the stone on your way out. Those capstones. Oh, he chiselled at them you can be sure. A quiet man, said little on any of that.

Every summer then looking . . . looking at the stalks . . . looking at the sky . . . light windy days we loved but not the dull cloud and the fear of that awful smell when the leaves curl up and the stalks shrivel, black. *Tá an dubh orthu*, they'd say, the old ones. But enough about that.

He worked away with the chisel down in Massey's Yard. Kept him going. Never a visit to the brother. You know well – why. He had us and couldn't bring home the *galar. Fan amach ón ngalar*, you'd hear them say. Mind for the plague! An excuse? Maybe. Sure who visits here? The Guardains, holding their noses. All right, all right, ye're not the worst!

Young Matt took it up from him. There'll always be need for a mason, no matter what the pittance. I moved on at ten or eleven. Working the spade! Staying with this one and that. *Spailpín.* Until I arrived at Mrs Quin's. Young Jimmy and I of an age so we got on. I found a *bothán* nearby where no one else would live. Afraid of the plague. And funny 'twas never knocked. It seems they left before the battering ram.

My mother's favourite tune, you know, the 'Battering Ram'. A great jig with a fearful name. A lonely jig when it's played right. She'd dydle it for us as she washed the clothes, *Um da-dil-um doo-dil-um di-dil-um daa*. Those times. Kneeling there by the bank of the *sruthán*.

Where was I? I settled in with my few pots and pans. And it was good enough. Unusual in that? I suppose I was. Most would stay in the house or shed but if I found any old spot I'd stay on my own. That bit independent, whatever it was. Young Jimeen and me off to the odd house dance or a few drinks below in the village. I think Mrs Quin was cagey of me, that I'd lead him astray! But she saw him off in the end, I hear. Off to Australia with his few pound. They said I'd have drank my share. That I never got. I swear. Do you hear the bell? *Listen*. It's time for the supper. Oh meal indeed! But it keeps us here. They'll be on to help me down. That's the way I am now.

The chalice be damned.

Not gone? I thought you'd left. The ward will soon fill up. Are you not afraid, of what you'd catch? Aren't you the brave one. Mother? Yes . . . When I'd go back for my few days at the end of the year, having worked for whatever farmer, I'd always stop by the river, a stream I suppose, where she used to bring us when she'd be washing the clothes. The *sruthán* was all we ever gave it. And now that you've brought it up, I can see it there as it was. Bubbling down the side of the hill. A long time since I laid eyes . . . My mother was ever . . . They say you never forget, your mother, and do you know what, it's true. Going back in the winter I'd always stop first at that little river, for some reason I don't know. Memories, I suppose. Oh, she was great, the mother . . . Ah wisha now, you've brought me back!

★

Johnny Bradford! Say hello to Johnny. But he won't come in. Always out here by the water tank, he'll drink his mug of tea and then be off. Mornings, after emerging from the County Home. Onwards he must go. A drover to the last. With his stories of droving cattle. Even in Scotland. Imagine that. Tall and lanky with the drooping moustache. Johnny'd been a drover, one of the last.

My mother smiles at the way he says 'the Work-house', spits it out. With a rasp. He'll never call it 'the Home'.

Off then with him towards Rathkeale. Swinging the blackthorn.

★

My mother used to say there was food all right, but they shipped it out of Cork and Queenstown. Soup kitchens then but you'd have to change your God – the way she put it! – so they preferred to starve, or come in here to die. THE ENGLISH LEFT US TO DIE. All right. All right, I'll quieten. But that's the way she told it. That or take the ship. And big farmers – you know the ones – took hold. With many a grabber . . .

Down by that river, each year on my way back. And Matty, the father, would joke about my find. 'A deal of good it did you! A deal of good!'

★

A voice emerges after the short lull. As if to cap it all, here outside Reilig na mBocht, The Famine Graveyard, duly named – by a committee – where all sorts of famines are intertwined, overlaid, bundled in. The voice begins in spring-song eternal:

O Mary, we crown thee with blossoms today,
Queen of the angels and Queen of the May.

The singer going back on his heels to reach the high note. All the while casting a glowering eye for anyone out there smirking.

And on it soars, with the chorus spontaneous. Does it resonate in the bones interred? Blossoms there are and it is May. Here with the priest, his blessing done, and the spectacled young orator, praising the committee – your new Guardians! – all volunteers who got little help from the Authorities, it seems, the spectacled man getting in his digs, and the first name buried here – the first recorded – is one Mary Lynch. Each in the crowd pictures Mary Lynch, 17 April 1841. We all picture our Mary Lynch. Poor Mary. And there is mention of you too, Paddy. Chalice-finder. Pauper. Buried somewhere in that field of mounds. Our Chalice finder.

It Was Noble Then

'Just give me the gun,' said Frank. 'Come on, give it over, you . . . you . . .' Then, bang! That was that. Bang-Bang the Dublin character couldn't have done it as well. Bang-Bang jumping out in front of the bus queue, steadying his index finger to aim . . . position . . . fire! Go 'Bang! Bang!' with the crowd responding, diving for cover, mortally wounded *mar dhea*. While some look on, demure. Above all that and sniffy. A good laugh in the really good old days. Rare oul times. But Frank was passed a revolver, a real gun, and he plugged poor man, the cop, Old Johnson.

They had passed the revolver one to the other not wanting to shoot, afraid now that the pre-arranged was staring them in the face. Too much written to order, this. Better if he hadn't shown, then at least . . . Donoghue went white it is said and afterwards had to be helped from the road. Puking, his hands trembling, all in a jitter. But Frank was made of sterner stuff. A rebel with a cause.

As in all of these cases there was the mind drill – more important than the wacky gun drill on the side of Barnagh: present arms, all that nonsense. More important than the firm boots for jumping dykes, the trench coat for the hours lying in ditches waiting for the patrol which either never came or came too strong. 'Fortified, no hope there boys, lie low a while, always another day,' as you gathered your half-frozen limbs and jaunted home or to the safe house. The mind drill, Frank went through it before we set off. It worked for him. Summoning up the past, the heroes of '98, the famine victims left lying in the grass.

Frank had all that and it stiffened his resolve. 'By God give me that gun.'

'Give me the gun,' Frank said, simple as that, and fired into Johnson's perplexed chest, one for the head as he lay struggling with shock and disbelief, there at the Cross Roads, a short trot from the town.

How did they get him there? A ruse. You might have guessed. Ah but you're too young, far too young to be listening to my rigmarole! His wife sick in Galway, *mar dhea*, came in on a telegram: 'Urgent, Come quickly.' In the know. The driver and all set up. Hackney. Broke down so soon. Must be the plugs. We'll have a look. No sooner stopped than out jumps our boys. Freedom fighters, thugs, rebels, gunmen. Subversives. Would-be heroes, latter-day saints, a blow for dear old Ireland. Ordinary men made extraordinary. And some just wetting their pants.

Old Johnson had many lives, was many people, depending on who's telling. A spy, to those who – take your pick – killed, assassinated, murdered him. Executed him, is that what your age group say! That lot you're hanging around with. Wouldn't I love to be as clever as ye! The eyes and ears of the people: the Royal Irish Constabulary, according to the lore. Nothing stirred without their knowing. A word in the ear and in no time at all it was above in the Castle, the Dublin hub, before Collins took them out. Then our boys got the bullet, strung up, houses burnt. So this Johnson, he was a spy, stood around the Square soaking up every tittle-tattle, especially after closing time and the porter breath let out half hints, spite at a neighbour came out, snatch of a song, enough for a lead, in Johnson's mind another note was taken, lick-arse to Dublin Castle, gave him an 'in'.

But others – drop the curtain, and now, raising it, here presenting, the new Johnson – portray a genial cop, dug into everyday policing of misdemeanours, a blind eye to the rising of the moon, not too taken with the Tans, and – whisper – a conduit to Don Flynn, Commandant Don Flynn, IRA commander, who cursed this sad adventure and swore that all actions in future pass through him. 'Orders for fuck sake mean something.' And not like the good Flynn to curse but this time he did. 'The bloody fools,' he is meant to have said. Depends who's telling.

What happened the Carnegie? I'll tell you what happened the Carnegie and the fine building he sponsored here off the Square – a Scotsman, of all things! – doling out largesse, and 'twas burned by the RIC and Tans that night after Johnson to deprive the citizens – if such there were, under the Crown – of their Carnegie Library. £5,000 it cost back in those years, imagine, and that not enough they then went after Ó Dálaigh the chemist as he was Sinn Féin, enough said, and the creamery too got the torch.

'The town was eerie quiet,' Proud Maggie Lane said to me, though the same lady had her tea box there on the shelf with the Queen, for all to see, thereon emblazoned. Thereon? That'd be her all right! 'Those July nights in 1920 were eerie I'll tell you,' Proud Maggie folding her arms at the door and looking into the distance.

The reprisals gave it legitimacy – up pipes the Analyst. We'll silence the Analyst, bang-bang! Your age group with your books.

They gathered at the monument on Easter Sunday morning for the roll call of the Old IRA, a nomenclature bestowed on past-it rebels, remembering the fallen.

'We are gathered here today to remember those who gave their lives that we might live in freedom.' He cleared his throat as a few Mass-goers stopped for a gawk. The Tricolour was raised and crows in the chestnut over the Arra gave an approving squawk. '*Squawk!*' Hovering over their refurbished nests, another layer to bed down the past.

Seán a Chóta stopped at the gate, leaning on the bicycle that he never cycled. He walked the bike home each day from the paper shop. A kind man – if from the Fianna Fáil side, my mother had to concede. The message bag hanging on the handle bars. The loose-fitting, long dark raincoat. The hat.

'Aye, those were terrible times. They came in and broke up the printing presses. Poor Byrnes was livid. After he setting it all up. That was the *Observer* gone for a while! I suppose we got under their skin a bit. With all the writing!'

His own skin was parchment white against his dark attire. And when my mother had gone back to clipping the hedge: 'You know I stayed a while when we were on the run . . . with your father's people. You don't remember him of course, your father. And what age are you now?'

He moved off slowly down the road. An old soldier, the pen being mightier than the sword, living out his life among old papers, in the teetering newspaper shop. Walking the bike out home.

And what is more these men did not lower themselves to those modern killers who masquerade as freedom fighters. Freedom fighters my hat!' He was warming up. 'No, my friends, the Old IRA that we here commemorate did their duty with pride and fought that we might be free. They did so with honour, with . . . with *pride*, unlike, *unlike . . .*' And he reddened while the words became stuck in his windpipe. An encouraging clap from those assembled, with the murmured, 'Sound man Dan. Sound man. *Maith an fear, maith an fear . . .*'

'It is wonderful, *a Chairde*,' he recovered, 'to see the relatives of many of these heroes here before me. You may well be proud that those who went before you and whose names are here inscribed carried out their duties with dignity. They did not lower themselves to the present day "bomb and the bullet" with their post-office robberies. They did what they had to do for you and me.' His voice was wavering again. 'Different times, yes . . . But noble men. Noble men, who did not shirk when Ireland's call was greatest.'

The crows cawed in the chestnut.

'Now, sadly to recall, some of the names inscribed here died in the Civil War, that most awful time, *a Chairde* . . . and we are here, both sides now here together, standing here at this monument, to heal those wounds. Aye, *a Chairde*, those bad times best left in the past.'

The crows settled back at their nests.

Paddy Power is entertaining us to a ditty he has picked up with the RAF.

'Home from England, Paddy? Never knew you could sing!'

I like the brandy cos it makes me randy,
but give me the good el vino,
The vino supremo!

'Good on you Paddy. Better to keep it down a bit though. Never know. Ger over there buys that *Phoblacht* every week. Never know, that's all I'm saying.'

'Fine for you lot.'(Paddy's accent has become tinged from being across the water. Hardly gone four years.) 'You had your schooling hadn't you and the chance of the Civil Service. Right, Pat? Me, I left at fourteen didn't I? Off to England, no choice. No one helped me get into the RAF. No pull there, not like here, all the time who-you-know, not much good when you come from the back of the Home. Bloody fighting the English? Where would we be without the English, tell me?' Paddy's getting a bit loud. Another song Paddy.

That's it. Now we'll move on. Come on Paddy, me boy, you'll be right. Right as rain in the morning.

Best man to write a composition. We'd pass it around from desk to desk – that good. Back in sixth class. But for all his brains he would soon be off. Gone from us after the dance down in Shanagolden. On the bus home we said our good-byes. Fourteen . . . fifteen . . . ? Was he even that. Our pal in the RAF. Rat-a-tat tat.

Pádraig, my neighbour, stops me in the street, eyes blazing, he's back on the tear. 'All over the world they're glued into it . . . this Forsythe whatever . . . can you imagine what that'll do? The whole world watching the same thing.' He leaned in nearer with his whiskey breath. Enveloped. 'They're leaving my school above there, leaving in droves, and you, young man, are off with that new crowd thinking ye'll change the world! Watching the Forsythe whatever all over the world. There's your imperialism!

'In one day, do you know how many cars passed on the Limerick Road? Go on, take a guess.' He's measuring commerce, counting the traffic. Over at the Cross looking out his window I suppose, those months when he's off it and bright in sobriety. 'Why would I be chasing around with that other' – he laughs – 'that other lunatic Hogan getting them to vote Labour? They'd prefer to be below roaring in front of the monument! Up Dev! Up Collins! And I watch their children leaving my school the minute they hit fourteen, heading away with the cardboard suitcases.

'They're all watching this Forsythe – "saga" is it? – all over the world! Do you realise what that'll do?' I have no answer. There is no answer to full-flown alcoholic reality pouring forth on the sunny footpath. The rattle of the bottles in the bag. A few days and then it blows over. Back teaching for the Emigrant Ship, the Bád Bán. 'Don't mind your Irish Brigades carrying flags into battle all over the globe. Wrap the green flag round me boys! Vote for the worker, my eye, they'd run you out the gate, set the dogs on you' – the laugh was burning out – 'with that other mad hatter Hogan. As mad as myself the poor man!'

On good days, walking past us when as children we played out on the road, he'd conjure sweets from the branch of a tree. Magician. 'Look, empty hands. Tell me can you see anything there? There you are, nothing, check the sleeves, now let's see which tree might have something for us, which tree,' – and swish, swoosh, he brought the pastilles! From a cluster of ash leaves. How did he do it?

We part with him shaking his head at a lost cause. 'They'd prefer to be shouting below in the Square about "free the North" and "we'll get rid of the border" with their "vote Fianna Fáil" and "vote

Fine Gael". "We'll get rid of the border and get you a house when the houses are built!" Live horse, you might say! Get you a ticket for the boat, that's what they might as well get.'

'Look fellas,' says Paddy, 'I'd wear the Poppy *and* the Easter Lily.'

'Come on, Paddy, time to go home.'

'The Poppy *and* the Lily,' as I pulled him out the door.

You never heard that? Well there you are.

Rock-a-bye-baby-on-the-tree-top! They've picked up the child. The Tans are all over the town! The drunkest of them is waltzing around the kitchen with the baby in his arms. You'll have to go down.

—Your name? What's your name?

—Mike Donoghue's my name.

—That's interesting. What a fine name he's got, chaps! *Mike Donoghue!*

(The child was back crying in the cradle.)

—You can't take our Mike, he's just home from England. What can he have done to ye?

—We'll soon find out what he could've done! Come on, Mr Donoghue! Tell us all about Old Johnson.

All night he's gone until she hears a thud at the door whatever time it was . . . after dawn. Thrown there in the doorway, a bundle of blood. All for a name. Lived on a few days. Called out in no roll of honour. Not 'active', they said. Mistaken.

So now for you, never heard that one? Well there you are.

Acquiescence

Tadhg felt light and airy coming home from the Advice Office. The window of the Cortina fully down; the breeze was warm. When his tangly reddish hair was cut short he looked the dead spit of his father. Believed in work. Getting ahead. There up ahead now was the father-in-law swinging his stick.

'God, he's some gligeen,' Tadhg scoffed to himself, 'swinging the blackthorn like he'd be droving cattle off to the fairs he's always on about.'

'Howa Jim! Will you hop in?'

The old man looked a bit startled at first and then quietly crossed the road to the passenger door and got in.

'Great morning, thank God, Tadhg. You'll be wynding up the hay above in the fort field I suppose. It must be fit . . .'

'Not ready for baling yet. The forecast is good. I'll bale this evening.'

'Wisha I don't know . . . but I saw a great flock of crows gathering at the priest's house. A bad sign when you see them boys gathering . . .'

Tadhg only laughed softly. The old man gave him great amusement.

'He's pure cracked!' He'd say to his wife Kitty. 'Wait till you hear what he was on about this time!'

And he'd go on about some remark old Jim had passed on the weather, or the cattle. He'd go red in the face recounting the incident, knocking great merriment out of it. Kitty usually smiled and would say something like: 'Ah, go on, you shouldn't be drawing him . . . you're a terror.'

But she was often silently hurt by his remarks on her father. After all, he had handed on the farm to her while the only brother, Jimmy, was off at sea working on big liners as a radio officer with no wish to come home and settle. The father had given him his choice and there was no bitterness but she always felt a great debt to her father on that account. To hear Tadhg mock him was hurtful and highly ungrateful. Old Mosseen, Tadhg's father, you can be sure wouldn't be so fair. Him with his big well-drained farm beyond in Reenbeg. All left to Dan, the oldest. The only thing Tadhg got from the same Mosseen was the mad fit for work. Couldn't leave a sod unturned.

For all that, she had great regard for her husband who never put her down and always tried to be kindly. She just wished he wouldn't go on about her father. She often hoped, in those moments after going to bed, when they'd chat back on the day, that he'd say some good things . . . Acknowledge the debt they owed her father . . . Say how glad he was to have got the farm . . . But she never cajoled it out of him.

And the wish grew deeper in her for an acknowledgement as time passed and she could see her father grow old. The articles on Irishmen that appeared in the Sunday papers from time to time were of little consolation. 'The Irish male is reticent when it comes to declaring his love . . .' or maybe 'Irishmen leave a lot unspoken, hoping the undercurrents will be picked up . . .' She'd ponder over such telling sentences there at the kitchen table and for a while those articles had appeased her, but not lately. Damn it, he was *her* father; Tadhg had fallen in for all of this so easily . . .

Arriving in the farmyard, the old man delayed before opening the door.

'I don't know, Tadhg, but that field was always slow to save. Whatever kind of grass is in it, it was slower than any other field. There could be rain before evening you know . . .'

Tadhg gave his easy laugh, opening out his door. 'Come on, we'll have a cup of tea.'

They just had the bare cup, nothing with it. The

dinner would be on the table at one o'clock (Tadhg had brought that routine with him). No dilly-dallying. Often in the old days they'd start at something and not eat until it suited the rhythm of the work. There was never any great rush.

Tadhg explained to Kitty how at the Office he'd got all he needed to know on draining the fort field and clearing up the place. He'd make it into a fine spread, suitable for silage next year. She wanted to know if they'd said anything about the fort.

'Sure what do they care?'

He winked to hush her, as he saw her father coming back in having been out watching the sky again.

'Will we take a walk up to look?'

As if looking at it will do any good, Tadhg thought to himself. But he set on up partly to humour the old lad and anyway he wanted to sharpen his appetite for the dinner. They had a half hour to kill.

Sure enough he was an entertaining old devil for as they passed the little pig house that led to the fields they disturbed a dry cow-pa and out scurried a black beetle.

'A bad sign when you see them boys out, Tadhg, mark my words.'

That tickled Tadhg enormously. Then he mentioned the big fair in town long ago and the day he walked the full twelve miles with two heifers (this one Tadhg had heard a few times before), two of the maddest little bitches that ever was calved for they took him up every wrong boreen on the way so that by the time he took his stand at the fair he wasn't worth tuppence.

Jim laughed to himself, knocking great merriment out of the recollection.

'You know 'twas a day very like today, the same sort of heaviness. And when we put our heads outside the Central in the Square – we were after a good few at that stage, mind – well, it was coming down in torrents. It was there running in floods down the street. Tim Buick was with us – the man who took the heifers – red with rage he was, he had hay down, poor man!

'We ended up having to stay the night, those of us that had a distance to travel. We had Tadhgeen Flynn singing – your father would have known him.

'It was still at it the next morning so lump it or like it we had to set off. Of course the men who had bought cattle were in the worst position but I could make headway.

'I'll never forget the floods at Coolanoran Bridge. I had to wade through with the water up to my waist. Man the things people did those times! And talking to people afterwards there was a good few witnessed wynds of hay carried along with the flood . . .'

Tadhg looked at his watch when they got to the hayfield. It was nearly time to turn for dinner what with all the old man's chat and stopping every now and then at certain points of the story. Tadhg kicked up a few sops, saying it would be fit for the baler around six. He imagined a nice level field of silage. *Next year*, he thought.

Old Jim was over near the scrub of hazel and blackthorn that covered the fort, handling swaths of hay at various points. *He'll go on about starting straight into making a few hay wynds now*, thought Tadhg, *but I'll have to draw him on the fort.*

'God, if you wanted now Tadhg, we could make up a few here near the fort.'

'Yerra no,' cutting him off, 'no point in killing ourselves like that. We'll have the baler run around in the evening. Mind you, we'd have more air going through if the hedges were cut back and that place cleaned . . .' indicating towards the fort.

The old man hesitated.

'Well, there's that in it too . . . Maybe the hedges could take a trimming. I remember cleaning those dykes out . . .'

Before he could get started on that Tadhg drew him back to the fort.

'There's a sight of bushes in there blocking up the place . . .'

'Ay, the middle could be cleaned up. I remember my father ploughing inside in it. But, of course, he'd never touch the ring.'

The mention of his father and the sudden

thought of those gone before him fortified the old man.

'No, nor I wouldn't ever touch it. There's plenty land besides. None before us interfered with it. No luck, you know, Tadhg. Only bad luck to follow.'

It would take more softening, Tadhg thought, *before he would win him over*. In the meantime he'd convince Kitty. One way or another . . .

'God, look at the time,' said Tadhg, and they headed back to the yard.

On the way, it came down again about the fair day long ago and Tadhg amused himself at the absurdity of walking all those miles, wasting two days for the profit on two head of cattle. *Pure cracked*, he thought, *pure catmalogin cracked!*

While Kitty was clearing off the table they listened to the end of the news. (Old Jim *had* to have the news and Tadhg would be half listening, mad to be back out.) This day, lo and behold, who should be interviewed only John Mc Awley, the school caretaker in the town and renowned for his knowledge of local lore and all the good fishing holes along the Deel. Another case of pollution and a three-mile stretch wiped out.

'The students inside in that school,' announced the caretaker/fisherman, sounding as if trying to hold back tears, 'have a book by George Orwell called *Animal Farm*. Well, would Orwell have predicted that in this year of 1984 – that other book of his – for all his predictions, that we would have our rivers killed off, the fish, the waterhen, are they all to go? Is it to be production at all costs and let the rest of us go whistle?'

'Will you listen to the auld codger!' – Tadhg.

'Whist, whist up,' said Old Jim. And when the news had finished: 'You'd have to feel sad for the old bucko. Sure he loves his fishin'.'

'He'll be full of himself now – being on the radio,' said Tadhg. 'Those townies, some of them, have plenty time on their hands – out fishing when they could be at a bit of work!'

It blossomed up into a pet day. Jim gave up on talk of wynds; went to clean out the little piggery. He had commissioned two nice ten-week-olds from a neighbour, which he'd fatten for the end of November. It was the one area over which he retained control. (Tadhg didn't care a hoot for pigs anyway. He was all into dairying.) And of course the hens. He helped Kitty with the hens. Ever since his wife Bridie passed away, father and daughter would mind the hens and Jim cleaned the henhouse.

As for Tadhg, he was out in the front field trimming the hedge by the road. While he was hacking away it was the thought of silage and flat, level fields that was going through his head. The short chat he had had after dinner with Kitty wasn't satisfactory.

They had waited for the old man to go out to the piggery and of course Tadhg put his foot in it by gibing about that. He had noticed lately she got her back up easily when he remarked about the father. But he was only joking. No good, it was a bad way to start.

'He's off to his chores! We'll hear nothing but pigs when them two arrive.'

Kitty gave a faint smile.

'You were saying what went on at the Office. Does Berty know about the old fort?'

'Yerra of course. "Mind," says he, "you don't bring bad luck on yourself!" And he giving a big scort of a laugh – you can imagine Berty! But he agreed 'twould make a great job of the field. And we'd be eligible for the grant. Berty'd see to it.'

'Aren't they supposed to report on a place like the fort . . . ?'

'God, you're as bad as the auld people for the fairies! Sure what good is it anyhow, a clump of bushes. And didn't Ryan go over it with the metal detector. A donkey shoe was all he found! I'd say something if there was a chance of anything in it.'

'Oh I don't know, Tadhg . . .' She braced herself: 'Dad would go mad, you know. He never let any-one touch it.'

She found herself getting a bit fiery.

'Oh let's not talk of it now, Tadhg.' And she switched to the hay. Shouldn't he hurry up and bale it?

Almost to defy them, he was now out with the briar-hook letting the day pass. Look at the lovely day! Himself and the beetles! He tried to jollify himself. But the feeling of confrontation had beset him. Flattened 'twould be and a fine field of silage would grow there next year. Then they'd see he was right. The place was his. They'd not best a Murphy. He hacked madly at briars and nettles.

That evening the baler arrived and the hay was made up. Some of it, especially near the fort, was hardly fully fit for baling.

'Carry on, Bill,' he said to the contractor, 'take it all in. Some of that will do for bedding.'

And with his great energy he was stooking the bales almost as fast as they bounced onto the field out of the machine. *Next year*, he was thinking.

At supper time he couldn't resist a few gibes about the weather.

'Well, the bales are stooked now and it can rain if it likes. Maybe 'twas a funeral them crows were gathering for Jim, what!'

'It's great to see it all made up, Tadhg,' Old Jim conceded. 'I hope them stooks are well settled though. The way the midges are biting outside we'll get a deluge . . .'

'Ay, them little fellows know better than the crows all right! The father often spoke of them, right enough.' He broke off with a chuckle.

The look on Kitty's face shut him up. He had a quick look at the paper. The television was useless during the summer. They got to bed early.

They had little talk that night. Kitty felt very uneasy. Tadhg had set out to best her father, she felt. And he had won. There was her secret love for the fort where she used to play when they were young. They had great games of hide-and-go-seek in the hollows, herself and Jimmy and the friends from around. And later on she would often go there on her own when she had some teenage problem on her mind. It was her retreat. Tadhg was going to knock that too.

God forgive her, but she hoped it would pour during the night. Come down in sheets like the day her father often spoke of and go straight through the bales. Teach him a lesson to be so cocky. Oh, what a terrible way to feel. Hadn't she brought Tadhg into the place . . . Her vows at the altar . . . She was restless and couldn't close an eye. *Rain, pour torrents on the fort field. Shield my secret place in floods.*

The Search

'Nolan!'

We jumped.

'If you don't put away those cards . . .' his words came slowly, slowly and deliberately, 'I'll go down and burst your head off the wall.'

I was mad. We had just got him on to dealing with the universe. He knew a few of us, at least, were really interested. Where does it all end? And time, what is time? He rattled us with that answer: relative to spinning planets. And Purgatory, Hell? Sir, do you think they exist?

'Well, don't you get hell here sometimes! From the other teachers, not me of course, right Nolan? Hmm.'

'The atom bomb, what's the *worst* thing, you ask. Well that booklet you refer to, sent around to every house . . .' he smirked, a knowing smirk. 'Well it's all right as far as it goes. You stock up on tins. Stand under a doorway if the ceiling starts shifting, hoping the lintel . . . And of course it would have to be well underground, we're not talking inches! Well, what does anyone think? The most important thing, if the worst happened?'

'Loads of beans, sir, tins of beans!'

'Beans, Nolan? Beans . . . wouldn't like to be down in that bunker with you then – the gas in this lab is bad enough!' Nolan was now happy as Larry, simple to get back in auld Dooch's good books: just show the slightest bit of interest.

Dooch would sit up there, his round form rarely stirring from the desk, the odd experiment, at a push, preferring to talk, make us wonder. Bunsen burners were for Inter Cert.

'So figure it out, what would you say is the most important thing you'd need in the bunker? Picture it, you're down there with your family or whoever.'

'Suppose it happened here, when we're at school, sir? Would we all go down to the basement?'

'Now you're talking *hell*, Nolan. Me stuck down there for weeks with you lot!' The laugh meant camaraderie. This was the way to spend a Friday afternoon in a double physics. Nolan had put away the cards down in the back desk.

But it wasn't Hell that worried me, kept me from sleep. It was God. In this Catholic school he was prepared to discuss it from time to time. Worried me when he explained the history of the Gospels.

And why didn't Christ write it down himself, make it crystal clear: this is it, A, B and C? Follow that and the job is oxo. Why leave it up to reporters, second hand, years later, not even there!

'But it all comes down to belief. In the heel of the hunt, it's down to belief.' If anyone reported back, the priests couldn't get him on that. Here he was toeing the line. Belief.

'Sir, do you believe we live forever?' – Nolan. 'How can anyone live forever?'

'Hmm. Well now that you've put away the cards, Nolan . . . Were you listening when we spoke about time? What does living forever mean if time is no longer there? Time as we understand it.'

'Ah, come on now sir. Come off it, hah?' Nolan getting all colloquial with him. 'Sure if there's no time there's nothing! Hah?'

'Well, there you are, how are we sure there *is* anything? Go and have a think about that for a while.'

After a suitable pause. (Nolan was rearranging the cards under the desk). 'In your maths class you may have heard your teacher mention Descartes?'

'The what?' from Nolan, under his breath. 'The cart? Oh . . . I have it! The cart before the horse! That'd be Mackey all right!' Great titter around the class.

Pretending not to have fully heard: 'I'll have no referring to other teachers in my class.' Dooch was getting his back up. Trust Nolan to push it too far. But the eyes went around. We settled.

'Well, our friend Descartes, he gave us the immortal dictum: *Cogito ergo sum!* Now you all do Latin so no doubt I don't need to explain . . .' (Dooch needed his bit of enjoyment too.) We all adopted as best we could the unbaffled look of the learned, but it failed Nolan as his gaze came up from under the desk.

'So, Mr Nolan, you'll give us the translation!'

Nolan gave some frantic digs into Collopy's back. With his head down behind him we could hear the muffled, 'Whassit, whassit, quick Colpy, whassit?'

'Eh, think . . . Sir . . . think.'

'Think what, Nolan?' A long and delicious pause. 'Oh for God's sake sit down. *I think, therefore I am.*'

Where was this leading? But the bell rang.

'You never gave us the answer, sir. Remember last week, the most important thing down in the bunker?'

'Nolan . . . the things you remember. Could you tell us about Faraday's Law if I asked you? Hmm? Well, the beans might get boring, no! And then, you see you all just thought of your stomach. What about the mind? How long could you stay down there without tearing each other apart? Games!

That's what you'd need. Loads of games. Even the cards, Nolan, wouldn't go astray. Chess, I'd recommend.'

'And when you'd come out of the bunker . . .' And on it went. Could you eat the vegetables? Wash them. What if the water . . . Getting tedious. You could tell on Dooch's face that we'd be as well stand out in it and welcome the hereafter. Find out sooner or later.

I got him back to the Gospels. We knew he did a few years towards being a priest. 'Well,' he said, 'it all seems to boil down to this: God . . . is love.' A bit of a titter. 'Not the love you look for down the back of the pictures, Hanly!' Hanly, milk-skinned and dreamy-eyed, always chasing the girls, gave a sheepish look across to his pal Dwyer. The conspiratorial look came back. 'No, theologians might define love more by what it is not: it is not about the self. It is the seeming contradiction: it is in giving that we receive . . . It is loving your enemy. If Greek hadn't been taken off the course you would have the basic word: *agape*. That is the beautiful word for it: *agape*,' he drifted off for a second.

'In here we learn that to every action there is an equal and opposite reaction, so that in giving away you should be doing just that, losing something, be diminished, but the Christian message is the opposite.'

Another day. Energy can neither be made nor

destroyed. He said to think about this for the week-end. Is every moment canned somewhere, like a reel of film?

The answer, Mr O Hagan, the answer. Questions, he tossed out questions. I wanted the answer. The only answer that preoccupied me. Was there, is there, a God?

So lying awake at night I'd go over things like 'to every action there is an equal and opposite reaction'. Take it out of the lab, he advised. So everything is balanced. Everything. No hill without a valley, joy without pain. But love breaks the mould. Love is ridiculous: giving to receive, love those who hate you . . . *Agape*, the way he pronounced it made it sound mystical, he made it sound kind in itself. There was the spreading word of flower power. San Francisco. Were we on the threshold of the Age of Aquarius? Was everyone thinking like me?

(There was something there to hang on to. The father figure had disappeared, then the surety of the priests. Now it was down to this teacher of physics. A certain excitement gripped him as he took control, broke the natural laws, thought of people who gave him a pain in the arse but he consciously tried to love them, they were his brothers, do good to them, otherwise the world was going to end in a bang. The United States and Russia, bloody fools, halfwits. The good ones, Abraham, Martin and John all took the bullet in the Land of the Free. What hope was there . . . But love was above it all. He felt himself rise above the hum-drum, suffer with the saints, go ahead, burn me in oil, crucify me, tear out my tongue but my mind will still love. Exhausted, he fell asleep.)

Nolan played *The Entertainer* nifty as hell on the piano there in the music room. We had it to our-selves quite often these days, the swots busy at their books and the smokers in their hidden nooks. Ragtime was all very well.

'Imagine falling into the abyss,' I said, 'the abyss of nothing.'

'Jeez, life's too short for that kind of stuff,' Nolan cajoled.

The staleness in the air. Everything seemed to have been said. We had got what we could from each other. Schooldays were ending.

'Wish I could play it like you, Nolsy!'

'Practice, old boy, practice.' Nolan was good at the toff accent.

'Getting back to what I said, *you* just don't worry about God: there or not? I don't get that. I can't get it out of my head. It's the only thing that bothers me.'

Nolan cleaned his glasses, all the while looking across at me with a goofy smile.

'What's the problem? You live, you die. Simple as that!'

He put on his glasses, giving him that Buddy Holly look, and he was back at *The Entertainer*, hunched over and speeding it up like a wizard. Morgan Traynor and his shadow Val O'Brien came in and said they had just got Barry McGuire's *The Eve of Destruction* so they asked Nolan to shut the fuck up with that *Entertainer*. Traynor was lord of the record player, bringing along his own needle in case his records got any scratches and never a loan from his record pile; play them himself and that was it. He carried a bit of weight, Traynor.

So we sat around and listened to more worrying stuff, agonising on the words. Were we hurtling to-wards destruction? Of course. But were the Powers listening? Of course not. Traynor's record spin-ning. Mesmerised, we listened as World War Three beckoned.

All these Superpowers, Superidiots, with their macho posturing, their bullying, while dreamy, make-love-not-war kids stuck flowers in their hair, went back to nature. That. I wanted that.

Your final word for us, sir , your final word?

'What can I recommend? Hmm, hopefully you leave here with a love of physics . . .' The titter went around. 'Hopefully, in the future, you'll keep ask-ing those questions.

'On Life? Hmm. When you're not reinventing the wheel, like us all? Oh I'd say when you have time, take down the Gospel of John.' A short silence and he began:

> In the beginning was the Word
> The Word was with God
> And the Word was God

'The word being *logos*. Write that down and, whatever about the physics, remember me for that! *Logos*.'

So he wrapped himself up in those words, their beautiful fall, the Word was all. In the beginning . . . was the Word. You could repeat that forever, it seemed.

This would be the booster rocket, to explode into the world and explain all. You were going to explain it all, dismantle philosophy and reassemble where everyone would have their grasp of love and flower power would rule the world. There would be no competition but people would only strive to improve themselves, sharing that improvement as if it were the community's, a part of the Word. Peace and love.

Back in the music room you were on a wing, not listening to the gibes, sailing out and into space, this love was an expanding fireball, for ever and ever engulfing what we choose to call the world;

beyond thought, beyond words – happy there, in that music room, as you set out to embrace.

The arrival at the door. With Nolan. The parting shot, the final bit of wisdom? You had rustled up a few quid from the ones who liked old Dooch's Friday afternoons, the languid style, the nod in the direction of syllabus, the hint of true knowledge. Whatever you bought was there in the wrapped up package. You arrived bearing gifts.

When the door opened it was . . . Dooch. But not as imagined. Dressed in an old sweater and dumpy jeans, he seemed a little shocked and out of it. At a door in the suburbs, a door we'd found hard to find. 'A present? But, but why? Come on in.' And his wife sat you down and there was an awkward silence. 'Just for all you've done . . . For the Friday afternoons especially . . .' 'Oh, thanks. Thanks for that. It's, it's a nice gesture.'

Come on, where's the banter, the subtle hints? The direction towards the future? Take on Kant and Heidegger? Square up to Nietzsche. No, Friday afternoons seemed to be gone, as in a flutter. A new class and new names, was that all?

We had tea and biscuits and said an awkward farewell. Dooch at home was a different ball game, but for Nolan he had, 'Whatever else you do, don't ever lose your sense of humour – when you lose that, you lose your soul.'

As he left us out all we got was: 'Don't expect too much, that way you won't be disappointed . . .' He seemed to see my face falling: 'And as for you, young man, you just keep up the search, right!'

He rose a smile at the door as we left. *Well now,* I thought, forlorn, *is that all we get in the end*?

No Return

Brenny English stepped down into the Corner Bar. Into the rattling good session, banjo and fiddle, at least one *bodhrán*. Festival.

'How's Brenny me auld pal?' this was from Grace with a welcoming smile. 'You're lookin' great, come here and give us a hug!'

'Gracey!' Still good-looking, still the pale clear skin and lively eyes. She was with a tall bloke.

'This is Tommy, you remember Tommy!'

Brenny remembered the face, drew in a breath to give a good look.

'Tommy, how's it goin'?'

'You're lookin' at me . . . no wonder, my first time back in years . . . Brenny? – Brendan, that's how I remember you, from school.'

'Oh, I was a few years ahead of you. Sure you're only a *gorsún*, Tommy! England?'

'Clapham Common! Where we all went in those years.'

And they got talking a little of work, how it had been for each. 'Sure, you know yourself – I have a daughter, twenty-three, Sophie. Split up for years but Sophie always keeps in touch. Doing great, not like the auld fella! She's even thinking of America,' proudly showing the picture. Meanwhile Grace is answering Brenny's eyes: 'Look, he's home for a while and we get along.' Tommy had other company at the bar and he said, 'We'll talk later on,' and hesitated. 'Brenny . . . I'll have to get used to your new name! You're staying here I take it . . . packed to the gills up town. Mind that woman there for a while!'

This gave Grace the chance to squeeze his arm. 'You're lookin' great Brenny – what're you on?' They had gone out for a short while when they were young, nothing too serious, but there was still the fondness, the 'auld *grá*', as Gracey put it.

The music hummed on in the background with the odd yelp when there was a change up in gear. There now you could hear the *Mason's Apron*, banjo solo. 'Ah sure, Billy's an absolute genius. An absolute genius – if he wasn't so odd!' Through the crowd Brenny could make out the cowboy hat bobbing and the pheasant tail feather, as always, stuck in the band, bright, saying, 'I'm here, banjo player.'

Gracey wanted to talk. The crowd pushed her into Brenny and he thought, with a slight guilt, the feeling wasn't unpleasant. But she wanted to talk about O'Neill. Oh God, anything but that.

'Out of prison I hear? After doing what? A few years. For all he done? That girl was right, fair play to her. If my poor mother only knew what he done to *me*. And she trustin him. "Oh, come on up any-time, Neddy. You can train the girls. Sure they're mad for the runnin'." If she only knew. Taught us more than runnin', the dirty auld bastard. What was I, ten or eleven? And he comin' round by the way helping us with our training – I was a good lit-tle runner you know!' With a wistful smile.

Brenny wanted to share his – felt he could with Gracey – but she kept butting in whenever he saw an opening. 'You know I had a kind of similar, not as—' But she was back again, the gin not letting her stop. Tears welled in her eyes. 'I'm only waiting for my poor mother . . . I couldn't while she's still alive. 'Twould kill the poor woman. To think she used to invite him in. Oh make tea, "Sit down there, Neddy," and Neddy this Neddy that. When I think of that slimy bastard and what he did.' She gripped his hand. But he too wanted to tell. To say "We're comrades, of sorts," to say somehow he might understand. He stood cradling his pint and couldn't but like again this girl who held on to a listening ear. Always the soft spot for her as she wandered from man to man since the marriage went. The anger he felt coming back from the

Men's when the box player returning to his seat should whisper: 'I see you talking to Gracey up there. You know what they're calling her now?' Here we go, some confidence, 'The village bike!' The scairt of a laugh. The shock of this reference to his one-time girlfriend, this offence, but he could only find words like, 'For fuck's sake, Jim. Ah, for fuck's sake go on out of it!'

'The worst time – tell me now if I'm upsettin' you, Bren, I know I've had the few drinks – I had to say it was barbed wire. That's what he got me to say. I caught myself in barbed wire.

'And my poor mother of course believes me. Giving out about I being such a tomboy. We ended up at the doctor. Seven stitches . . .'

'Did the doctor . . .?'

'Sure the doctor believed my mother. Didn't want to know if you ask me. How did it happen? I was climbing over the fence into Lacey's field, Doctor . . .

'Oh I was, climbing over a fence all right.' She clenched her fist. 'As soon as my mother's gone – 'twould destroy her – I'm going to go after him. I'll wipe the smirk off his auld crooked face. God forgive me I'd love to see him hanged.'

Donal was standing in his mother's doorway, benevolent family friend. 'Well, will you be down to us this weekend? You should see the work he did the last time!' He looked towards the mother. 'He made haycocks of the entire field, you know. The small field in front of the house. Saved it all from the rain while we were away at the wedding.' Should have made him proud as punch but this only revived a sad smile from young Brendan. In his confusion he heard himself say: 'Ah, I can't. I have a match . . . a hurling match tomorrow night . . . and we're training tonight' he rushed in, for fear even one night away might be offered.

'Ah well,' Donal saw through it, 'maybe we're getting a bit big for the farm, are we! You know you're always welcome. And yourself, Jane,' he addressed his mother, 'you're keeping well these times?'

'Pulling the Devil by the tail, isn't that it? Trying to mind myself! And your uncle, Mick, is in good shape?'

'Never a fear of that fella! Has to be out every day – half the time getting in my way!'

The car drove off. 'Now why wouldn't you go off down for yourself this weekend? I heard you say nothing about a match.'

'It's . . . it's training,' he conceded, 'we have training up in the Field.'

'Oh, I think you should make an effort. You used always love going down there to them. Your father and them were very close. Helped us out, too. They're forever talking of the day you delivered the eleven *banbhs* with that sow out in the flaggers. All on your own!' The praise brought back the faint smile.

'I know . . . but maybe next time.'

Next time and next time till there was no more calling and a slight coolness developed.

'Ah sure, he's growing up. Maybe he has a little girl distracting!' And that was that.

That sow he was sent for had a surprise. Lying there hidden among the feileastroms, she had begun to farrow, and now what? What, what should he do? He had seen it done once, snipping the cord back in the shed but . . . Shout. Shout again. So far from the house and now she gives a great heave and there it is, covered in slime, the first little *banbh*, now, oh now what? Slime on his hands he frees the mouth. Breathe little piglet, breathe, and now the cord, so tough between his nails, the slippery cord, but succeed he did and relief, now to put him to her teats and have him suckle, watch she doesn't turn and bite, he's heard of that, but no she's quiet and he settles in to delivering . . . eleven. There on his knees in the field. He counts them again. Proud sow, proud small boy, praise all round.

Not able to tell, unable to tell, even himself, something he locked away and got on blindly with life. But the adult world had left him down. 'You're one great little man. Now stiffen your muscles there. There on your arm. Ah, sure you'll make one strong man. Play for Limerick I'd say. Play for Limerick.'

The kitchen, darkening in the April evening. No, no need for light. 'Isn't it light enough we have. And how are you doing in school? Top of the class, I'll bet you are. And already playing on the Under-14s!' The rank breath of adult male which . . . the male breath too near . . . too near until Brendan goes SNAP.

'Brought us up the field. "Go away there now," he'd say to Mary Ann, "keep on jogging till I tell you stop. I have to show Gracey a few exercises." Exercises! In behind the trees, he took me. And it happened many a time. With my poor mother saying, "Neddy, come up whenever you like, sure you're doin' wonders with them. Ready for the Olympics they'll be!" and she'd smile at the two of us, Mary Ann beaming up: "Neddy says I'll be better than Grace. I'll be faster than Grace. I beat her again today." But I saved her. At least I think I did. She nearly ate me the only time I brought it up.

'Of course she was always a bit jealous of me. Jealous of my looks! What do you think, Brenny? Oh, sure we had good oul times, Bren, remember? My *looks* is right!' She lightened up. The crowd were making room for a set. Sure enough Grace was led out. Always game for a laugh, but she was able to dance. The polka set.

Not able to tell. How to tell? Then Brendan's mother had to go away for treatment, that time when the house smelled awful with drink and her friends cajoled her out the door. She screeching, 'I'm fine. I'm fine can't ye let me be . . .' and he had to stay with the neighbour, Molly Breen. Molly was great to him. Trying to explain how his mother would be well again, and we all had our crosses to bear, she'd soon be right as rain.

That offered a fine excuse. Had to check out the house, you know, in case there'd be any leak, check the gas, that sort of thing. And he said to Brendan to come along, but he didn't want to go, he knew from that day in the shed, when farm life came to an end, how Donal would never know . . . But he went all the same and this time it was 'Sit down sit down we'll have a little chat and the hurling you love the hurling now let's see how your muscles are coming along, flex them there for me till we see if you'll make the team.' The sun was fading, the kitchen dim. 'Flex them there till we see.' *There's something wrong but I don't know what* was running up and down Brendan's spine. Burning into his brain. Old Mick had opened his fly and was saying, 'Feel my muscles, my muscles there on my thigh, yours are nearly as strong, do you know that, young man, feel how strong mine are. You'll have muscles like that, that's it, go on, feel them. You'll play on the Limerick team.' He felt. Snapped. 'I have to GO,' getting flustered as hell, hopping up from the chair, 'I have a *match I forgot. I forgot.*'

And that was the end of that. Luckily enough. No more visits down there though Donal would call and he loved him like a lost father. But he couldn't go and he couldn't say.

'My poor mother, if it wasn't for her. You're great to be listenin' to me there goin' on. It isn't that many you know, will listen.' Gracey back from the dance. 'Am I glowing?' she said, looking into his face. 'Am I *glowing* like a queen!' she cocked her head and that smile . . . 'Horses *sweat* they say! Isn't that it! But listen, it was good to talk. I see he's getting anxious to go.' Brenny gave her one more hug, but she still didn't hear what he had to say, or how it might make her feel.

The Student

. . . so I might see you there, Joe. And, do you know, all this has forced me to reminisce. Of course you two had that something in common. You did your bit, I remember, to coax him along, in case he felt, what? Too alone? Bear with me as I bring my mind back. The hollow days – could they have been otherwise? – when I chose medicine; I think he resented that. No more 'Let us go then, you and I', when we bombed out a little on Eliot and Dylan Thomas. I had gone along with it. 'Listen to this, man: "Never until the mankind making . . ." Get it off by heart', he'd say, 'get it rolling along'. He liked how I did the Welsh lilt. But I soon had more than enough on my plate, in and out of labs, mixing with (to him, I imagine), a rather sedate lot. Yes, I think he sensed that and drew away. But you and he seemed to always get on. At least, that's how it comes back.

So here I am, Joe, on my afternoon off; Relief Doc couldn't come too fast. You'll forgive me if I indulge. Sift through the past. He nudged me towards Karl Jung and, for a while, you know . . . for a while we were away on a hack. Noting our dreams first thing as we'd awake. Comparing over and back. Those early days when we shared a flat. You could feel his excitement, analysing. And each night he'd have to report, all his bloody lectures, oh the full report, the whole whack! Remember he did *start* – if it wasn't to last.

Students are allowed play with words and we played. The nutty professor – we would come up with a better name in time – 'walked over and back, over and back,' he said, behind the lecture desk, so that those hell-bent on getting every word would be there craning forward, heads going 'over and back, over and back.' Mac Gee could read into his head: 'For oldsters like me it gets tedious, this professorship, but ignore that, I won't be meeting you lot in the bar.' And if, God forbid, they landed in his favourite snug? He'd probably pace up and down with his pint, 'Ye wouldn't believe now what I'm going to tell ye, and don't bother looking for them – Kavanagh, Behan, Myles, all gone – ye're too late, missed nothing, Mc Daids no more, piss off outa here to the Student Bar, outa here to the wild west of Belfield. The crack is over, ye might as well know.' Words like that.

Sheaves of paper curled on the lectern, the window open for the autumn breeze, he could be doing Carrauntouhill in his head, you wouldn't know with professors. Professors could hang from the ceiling, like bats, fold in their cloaks for the night, no notice, 'Sure isn't he a professor, a professor of literature, no less,' but too late for all that. Now Kavanagh of course . . . and Eliot . . . Oh Joe, were those the days, tell me now, were they what! 'And my whole world turns – misty blue', remember that? He'd play that over and over on the cassette, it seemed to get to him. And he'd get us to listen, have us take it in like 'Never until', insisting we take it all in as if somehow we weren't hearing what he was hearing. Weren't feeling what he was feeling. The exasperation.

Mac Gee eyes us with his tray, unsure if he should join, unsure if he should not join, but anyway, down he sits. 'Well Pat, how's the English Lit?' We'd string him along. 'You see the thing is this . . .' and off with him excited about some translation of Proust he had come across, give the auld 'R' a good roll there, go on! Then Hardy, Hardy for another while was his man. 'Ye should read his poems, skip the prose.' Wondering what to do with our days, our time, our lives. Had we lives? Were we any good? Were we mediocre? Mediocre. Out there was grey. Which reminds me, you were a bit of a Hardy man yourself, Joe, if I recall, even though you were ploughing into the German. Which reminds me.

Poor Neart. Poor Neart had it all to do. Whoever put Heinrich Böll on our Leaving Cert course
should be taken out the back and shot! Existential-
ism is bad, but try it in German, to a bunch of
when-will-this-all-be-overs, talking of girls,
fraulines we'd allow. Poor Neart, all eager, bringing
in these German magazines, bands, cool German
bands trying to look American; uh-uh Neart, nice
try but not quite . . . Except for Mac Gee, who got
carried away with old Neart's '*Es muss etwas
geschehen!*' Yes, Something must happen. There it
is in a nutshell. Neart had one believer. Böll and
his *Existentialismus*! Mac Gee was gobsmacked,
you remember. Maybe you too, Joe, may I say, in
your quiet way, you were taken in with it too. The
Existentialismus!

The student café is one long cold place of hair and
pretence, of swagger and hidden fears. Mac Gee's
father a taxi driver – hardly a boast now is it? What
with. Underlays and overlays of professions, of
wealth, even old dried up wealth – the veneer
being kept. So poor Jude the Unsure – for that's
what we called him now – kept coming back for
the knocks, all these faces around him were *sure*,
all of a mind, of a mind that Friday night was
theirs, that upward flights were theirs – leaves fell
softly on their front lawns – while poor Paddy was
juggling too many balls, and we kept tossing in one

more, here Paddy, you'll manage, go on! See them fall.

Where were we? Mac Gee would arrive: 'We have to be doing something, isn't that all there is? Something must be happening. Is that what keeps us alive?' He wanted to believe that stuff. Wanted us to debate. And if you were there, Joe, ye'd be back to old Neart with Mc Gee still loving the *Deutsch*, getting you to say it again for him, you being the expert now, *Es muss 'was geschehen. Es muss 'was geschehen*!

Of course, the meanness of secondary school could not be left behind, it had to be ferried into the dark corners between Theatre 1 and Theatre 2, floating spaces where bullshit pervaded, student twiddle-twaddle, which unnerved Mac Gee. I'm sure, Joe, he wished on many a day he was back in his father's car, cruising for a living, watching that woman with the heavy bags, ' "Watch this now, son, she'll wave us down, you'll see," driving about to put me in here!' Imagine, poor Mac Gee feeling he couldn't let him down but 'here' wasn't where he wanted to be. Where? He knew not precisely, just his innocent feeling of finding Kavanagh's ghost, rustling up Behan, discovering perhaps that his few poems could float, poems he had shown to no one – except maybe you, Joe. His father wouldn't comprehend, just wouldn't be into that, and these friends from school were back at the old slag, this wasn't what he was at, this was not it at all.

But for yourself, Joe, the others, the rest of us, laughed when he tried to convey, convey what but the sounds of those words. How could they mock poor Neart? 'He was a *teacher*, he *taught* us, I don't know . . . for me anyway,' he stumbled, '*Es muss etwas geschen* didn't it sound so urgent, so right, so "this is it", so "let's go, life"!' but all Paddy could get was a laugh, 'Yeah Paddy boy, something must happen you say, like attending a lecture for a change!' We saw him falling off and then the slagging eased back for we weren't that bad at heart, we knew his constraints . . . I like to think.

That time he took up with the Samaritans, helping the down-and-outs, coming in one day and this time more estranged, we noticed – almost, I would say, aggressive. I remember those words: 'Ye don't know anything about out there, ye're in here cocooned.' And he went on about how easy we had it. Easy now, Paddy, easy. You weren't with us that day, Joe.

There was the day he arrived on with the diminutive Connemara poet, his new hero. The Poet was all he was called, you got caught up with him too, Joe, am I right? 'He doesn't believe in this bloody place, look how he's done, with two books of verse, and none of these degrees . . . doesn't believe in it, "stifles", he says.' Mac Gee was all agog. A gas man The Poet, with limericks on tap, but serious as hell when readings came up; only your-self, Joe, could be got to attend. God, poetry read-ings must be bloody hard so that even The Poet himself ran off – am I right! – when his bit was done, over to the nearest bar, to quaff it back, to get the hell out. And Mac Gee all this time was there by his side, he'd found him at last! His guru, at last! Hanging off every word.

I think you were brought in on that – am I right there, Joe? – asked you to translate over from Ger-man. For The Poet. Someone obscure no doubt. And in the heel of the hunt Mac Gee got to do his poetry reading. His big night had come but then they attacked him because of the ones on the North. Another story! The Poet consoling: 'Hide back in the curled grass. You're a leveret. Stay still in the curled-up grass, for that's your world.' That was the phrase that came back. We all had it off. A leveret, our Pat!

Of course he got his head kicked in. Bound to hap-pen, with his Samaritan do-gooding and his quizzical nature, searching forever. And we were a bit jaw-dropped with his happy acceptance: 'These poor devils know no better' etc., etc. Getting his glasses repaired and a stitch in the nose, back again to helping out. 'How could we just sit there in the canteen? Something has to be happening.' He had stopped the German repeat, lost as it was on our newfound group, but for yourself, Joe, trying to nudge him along, 'Try a few lectures, Pat,' but no, he now had his friend The Poet, someone who understood, a fellow-mind, and the grant money went in Mc Daids, where his dreams could be left to reside. The Poet, being into nature, said it was like the hare's twist of hay, that delicate, there was no den or cave for the wandering lyric poet, but left to the form in the grass – The Poet seemed to love the hare!

'Of course,' says Mac Gee, 'the hare is hunted just like we were . . .' And then he'd get all excited about the North and how we were 'not even lifting a finger'. Did we not care, here in this barren canteen with the flat bare fields out there, as flat as our lives? He could get very carried away!

And how he'd tear into us about the way we treated poor Neart, that night at the concert, the 'going-away' gig. That was always gnawing away, even with time passing, he was still going back to it. 'He was trying to play the great old air, the *Cúilean* and the best we could do was jeer and mock. It was fuckin' awful, let's be fair about it, fuckin' awful.' Of course he loved Neart's Irish classes as much as the German and believed we should all be speaking the bloody thing! That and reciting Eliot!

Poor Neart. '*Ní neart go cur le chéile,*' he'd plead. 'Let that be our motto in this class, One for all and all for one! Isn't that it, lads?' But of course it wasn't it, not for most of us. Soft touch, that's what we saw. And that was how he got his name. Remember, Joe? *Neart*, meaning strength! What a joke for each new class, waiting for him to say it, the nickname passing down! Teaching Irish and German to the uncouth, 'See the way Ó Ríordáin plays with the words "*saoirse agus daoirse*" freedom and . . . well, non-freedom, *smacht*, see how the Gaelic with one change of letter brings opposites into play.' Lost on us of course. Except for Mc Gee and yourself maybe, hanging off every word. Freedom, we understood. Get the hell out of school and into the free world. Get outa there.

> They marched in the sun,
> in the cold, cold sun,
> for injustice done.

Bloody Sunday did for him. The way some of us saw no point in marching and slunk off into our lectures. Wouldn't take the day off. He was fit to be tied. How couldn't we see? These were our people mown down in Derry. 'Sweet Doire Cholmcille' almost reduced him to tears as he looked at us, bewildered. (I forget where you stood on that, Joe. If you marched?) And then. Oh then. The Poet lets him down. Whatever about us, he was despairing of us, but The Poet to scarper. That killed him. The poet not to march like a man with him, march like a man to the British Embassy and show them we'd take no more. It was then 'the sweet smell of smoke', which he'd duly recall, reminding us of how they burned it down, how he regretted none of it, 'the bastards inside looking out.' But The Poet ran. That got him more than anything. Oh, The Poet said Ó Bruadair and Ó Rathaile and all that merry band of poetic recorders would never be at the battle front. Their job to piece together the bitterness of loss. With polished words. But not to be one of the mob. If you ask me, that was when he was lost. The Poet was his saviour, his bulwark against our sterile reality of jobs, of steady-as-she-goes lives; The Poet for him was the rebel, the something happening, something being done, everything that we were not, but then he ran. His excuse: stand back and record, not be part of the mob. How could he come from that?

The Poet made up for Old Neart . . . until that. Old Neart he loved, yourself and himself. At least that's how I see it now. The very mention of Heinrich Böll! Not Heinrich to us but – Height-of-Bull. All we wanted was the bloody synopsis but Mac Gee and yourself would go on. About this *Existentialismus*! The pair of ye getting carried away.

What I'm dying to know now is this: did ye keep it up, the friendship? You left college to us and quietly went off in the bank; the *bank* and you, Joe? That I could never figure out. So when poor Mac Gee's name came up I said I'd chase you down.

Ye must have met over the years. Ye must have kept in touch. This news of Mac Gee has brought me back.

We'll have to meet up for a chat.

Geronimo

'You go on over first.' The voice was harsh. I hesitated: he had the gun. This friend, this middle-aged, this good, chuckling friend, my neighbour, wasn't there. Like he had died and we revived the corpse, made it walk, gave it talk. But not Johnny, not my friend and neighbour, Johnny Behan.

I went ahead through the gap, hoping the gun wouldn't fire as he came after me through the ditch, throwing a leg over the barbed wire. A sense of relief as I landed in the Low Field, and I moved on quickly. What were we to find? Would he be satisfied now with a simple explanation? Bizarre, no doubt unusual, but look, that's how it happened. To lose two bullocks in one night was a bad blow, an awful blow given the state he was in, the bleakness he was travelling through.

'Well,' I said, trying to cheer him up, 'you're as nimble as that goat, do you know that.' Only a hint of a smile and the eye contact – as always these days – could mean anything. He was definite it was deliberate and what's more he was definite who did it. That crowd down the road.

We walked over to the drain which came out through the field – a one-time attempt to draw off the wetness from the Low Field – and soon were standing over the marks on the bank where they had rolled in. You could still see where they'd lain, close together. The reddened earth, from the struggle in the dyke. Two in the one night.

'I know, Johnny, it's bloody bizarre but that's probably what happened. They lay down near the drain and rolled over during the night. On their backs, unable to struggle out. I know two in the one night . . .'

He was in his own world. 'The bloody bastards, they're always trying to get me back, ever since I ran them.' He stared into the feileastroms growing near the drain which the mower didn't catch. 'We'll have to cut them bloody flaggers and clear it up. What do you think?'

He was moving about not needing an answer. Why the gun hugged to the chest? He couldn't think I had anything . . . 'The bloody bastards, I know they were behind it.'

I was glad to hear him repeat 'the bloody bastards', to be still on his right side. And I knew the history, thought I knew. Family farm where the sister got nothing, having married beneath her, defying the father. Cabbage going missing, potato drills dug up at night. All blamed on them. Who knows.

'We'll head on back'. Jesus, the relief. But now the gap to be manoeuvred one more time. 'On you go,' he says with resignation. I move fast. Down. Watching the gun in his hand as he came through, staying out of its aim just in case. And we trudged home forcing a conversation. Only the bare replies.

'That's where he hid when the Tans came in, I often heard my poor mother tell, in that small press!'

'And he seems a big man in that photo?'

'Big, is it? Twice my size!' he chuckled. 'Twice my size if the picture's anything to go by! Look at him. Head and shoulders over Mullins, the two of 'em with their pistols, full of bravado! They say 'twas taken in front of the castle, around the time Collins passed through going down to Cork.

'You can read it there, what it says on the back, that's it: *Pádraig Ó Beacháin, Lios Rua*. That's about it as far as my Irish goes, *Lios Rua* – the Red Fort, that's what I heard at school, isn't that it, our Lisroe? That and my name, *Seán Ó Beacháin*. You'd hear that every morning first thing for the roll call and you'd shout back, *Anseo*! After all poor Padge there fought for, smiling out at us not knowing how soon he'd die. It could do with a bit of a cleaning.

'But anyway, Padge – he got himself curled up in there in the flour bags. That used to be the flour press, all homemade bread that time, and the story was around of how, over in Athea, they bayoneted the flour bags! Out of spite, of course, but that night they just opened the small door and moved on. Checked the rafters and everything, every damn thing but not there. By the time they left of course – and they left cursing and blinding, she used to say, but they didn't do too much harm – he was like, what's this they call it? Rigore . . .'

'Rigor mortis!'

'You have it! They had to uncurl him there on the kitchen floor after being wrapped up for so long!'

'Houdini! But imagine, if they had bayoneted the flour bags . . . Jeez, the thought of it . . .'

'There'd be no bread for a while! That's for sure.'

The great white puck goat peeped in the door. I went to shoo him back to the yard. But Johnny says, 'No, leave him.' And then he starts his conversation with Geronimo, for that was the puck's name.

'And how are we today, Geronimo? Why aren't you down the land minding your herd of cattle, Geronimo? In here for the calf nuts, is it? "Oh, just a handful, old boy. Boring work with those stupid cows. Nothing but gossip." Go on, throw him a fist of it.'

Going down the fields for the cows at milking time, Geronimo would follow on, pucking you from behind, Move on. A character, that goat.

We'd enact our mind-plays in the kitchen or in

the cow-house, giving Geronimo leading roles and a deep authoritative voice for his witty comebacks. We'd place him in Westerns where he would shoot out the varmints, more times in Chicago taking out Al Capone. Or sometimes he would predict the weather. Johnny's way of indicating next day's work. Things he wanted you to do but mightn't be able to ask, leaving it to Geronimo. But rutting season came and he headed out to Ardagh where – reports came in – he attacked an equally magisterial opponent in the front-door glass of the church. We missed Geronimo.

What in the fuck got into us I don't know, but we squeezed in the bedroom window and saw the squalor. The room he always kept locked. The rank ... But idiots that we were we hung any old clothes we could find off hangers, not much, but he'd know someone had been in. Hilarious when you're pissed. And to make it worse he didn't ever refer to it until now, in this dimness. The good being long gone out of it.

''Twas yourself and Corduff, am I right? Ye're some pair. Ye were in, however ye got the key!' this seemed to be in jest but I knew the wrong. Some things go too far.

'In where Johnny? Not a hope, it's dreamin' you are!'

He moved on to heavier matters. 'She's sayin' that it's my child. That's what she's at.'

'But Johnny, she's your niece, ah she can't be saying that. Come on, sure that child is grown. She's never that bad.'

'That's what she's sayin',' he broke in. 'They're all at it. They have it all over the town.'

'Ah, they're not, don't be botherin' yourself with that.'

They're all at it behind his back. There's all this talk. This talk in his head. He sees it in the way they look. And they killed two of the herd. Rolled them in. For sure.

Almost dragging him under. But the neighbours eventually moved and with quiet coaxing the gun was taken in and he agreed to a spell inside.

'The Snake Pit!' was how he'd refer back to it when he found himself dwelling on those days, the humour returning, but lukewarm, not like before. The Snake Pit and the chuckle.

Yes, but not quite. Not quite. With the tablets rounding off the edges, our Johnny had become a watered-down version.

The cigarettes and all the other stuff, in the end, bringing him down.

'So you must have been frightened then that evening! When you went out with me and I having the gun!' Good to be able to talk back on the dark days but your voice is weakening, the tough roundy frame dwindling.

Final days when cancer moved in to eat away

from inside, final days saw you move off quietly. Haymaking – gone. Milking – gone. Checking for mastitis – gone. The unctuous movement of prayer in a sterile house, being looked after till the final collapse. A child's corpse. '*What the fuck was it all for?*' I would love to have heard you roar. Search for some meaning. Geronimo. Speak through Geronimo that we may hear what hints you have for tomorrow, what chores lined up, what hints for hereafter. Go on, let us hear.

Why the quiet graveyard, back with the old people, the swashbuckling uncle killed by his own having survived the Tans, the John Bull-hating father, the poor hard-worked mother, why enclosed by it all? The farm in autumn drooping, heavy with all the past.

Geronimo! Geronimo is at the door. Speak through him. *He stands there resplendent.*

'Do you know my biggest regret? Years ago when I was on the liquor, before the farm was handed over, I sold an old ass to that good-for-nothing down the road. Money for liquor, of course! And then one day as I was coming home from the creamery there was my poor old ass being driven into the ground by that brute with a stick. I regretted that. I arrived there in the yard and I just stood there thinking back. D'you know that? I couldn't bear to go in and face the mother. D'you know what I'm sayin'? Even though she'd say nothing.'

'She'd be out there milking the cows and then he'd arrive home from the fair, the money spent, bawling about John Bull. That's all he ever did about John Bull! Bawl about it on fair days with my poor mother there under the cows, milking her lot, then his, while he slept it off, cursing there by the fire.

' "You'd think 'twas John Bull himself killed your Uncle Padge," she whispered to me once with her shy smile. Apart from that she never had a bad thing to say of him. Blamed it all on the drink. But 'twas her did all the work except for his *buaileam-sciath* during the hay. He'd have to fork more than the rest. You'd have a *meitheal* of men and he'd have to be there ahead of 'em, cock of the walk.

'And do you see that fellow there in the bowler hat? That's right, the grandfather. He was said to be worse again. All the men . . . Oh, I don't know . . . I'll have to go back to the Home! That's all I'm fit for!'

We'd both get a kick from that, Johnny's eyes pinched with laughter. *Standing there resplendent at the Pearly Gates a great white goat awaits his master.*

The wet days, looking out at the rain, our door to the north, like the wren from her nest. And he'd be there saying, 'Worse than a sore arse, that rain. Will it ever cease?' and then with the laugh: 'Take me back to the Home! That's all that's for it.' But we had a visitor, his monthly visit.

'Not if you were to throw it out the door! Put away that teapot. I'm telling you, don't go making tea. 'Twill go out the door, I tell you.' Our visit from Danno the court clerk. Never accept a drop or eat a bite. Up and down he'd walk with the odd break on a chair, then up again. Hands behind the back, half in a trance as he recited each case for us. Of course we'd be sitting there, rapt!

'They were up again this week, the Cotters. The Turpentine Cotters! You'd think they'd have their lesson after being caught, for the TB scam and all the rest, but not a hope of it, they're back again.

' "Is it yourself George Cotter before me again today?" Leahy the Judge, but not half as witty as the last man, Quille. "Mr Cotter? Hmm? I thought we had dealt with this case?" Out from under the eyebrows, giving the quizzical look down at me! "The heifer, I believe – in farming parlance – that doesn't take to the bull is called a repeater. Is this what we have here, Mr Cotter, a repeater?" The court was in stitches.'

As he got into the detail Danno would focus on the kitchen floor, Sheppie moving off from his favoured spot to allow the swinging gait to go forward and back from doorway to table, concentration everything – bringing on full recall.

Johnny enjoyed it no end. Chuckling away and winking at me behind Danno's back as we savoured the lingering details of courtroom procedure. The town buckos who gave as good as they got. ' "And is that all, your Honour? And thanking you, your Honour!" From Cotter, tough as leather,' says Danno. We might as well be inside with them, that good.

Finally, exhausted by his eloquence and procedure, Danno would make to leave as entreaties rose up again.

'Not if you were to force it down my throat! Not a drop, but thanks, sure thanks very much.' Waving it away with the hand. Then off.

So standing there resplendent at the Pearly Gates a great white goat awaits his master: took you a while, old boy! The last word going to Geronimo.

Fog

'Where're we going now, lads? Hah!'

From the seats behind them a sudden interest. He answered himself.

'Into the fog, lads, that's where! If it doesn't lift soon there'll be no game. Down here! In this god-forsaken place by the estuary . . . there's always fog down here if you ask me. I don't know how they live here. Hah!' He tossed his head back – that gesture which said 'I give up on them.' *What? You can't hear? A child's voice? Of course you can't. How could you? We're on a bus, the rattling. Of course you can't hear.* Usually cars, any old jalopy to take a bunch of us, the boot stuffed with the jerseys, black and white of the Magpies. Up the Magpies! Come on the Magpies!

A small man, the trainer, not much taller than us under-twelves. Who are we playing? Ask Miney, he'll know, his father knows everything. Their shop full of leather smell, footballs, harness and sliotars.

Counter worktop there in front of you. 'Mind that sliotar now, your mother there can't be out buying you a new one every time ye hit it into the hedge. And every night rub in the Vaseline in the grooves, d'you see, young man, and what do you rub into your hurley every winter? What did I tell you? Linseed oil. Am I right?' Always right was Mr O'Toole, Ted-the-Harness, kindly enough but always the stern advice. In his coarse brown work coat. 'Mind now your mother can't be forking out for sliotars every day.'

The first puck of that ball in the backyard, the clean smack off the ash, the solid feel in the hand. Whack. Rebound. Whack. Football nowhere near it, hurling was the game. Any big *geochach* could push his way around at football, elbow into the mouth, but hurling was swift and clean. Smack, it's up the field, smack, it's back down. Clash, the clash of the ash. The ball going where it will.

'Mind how you look after it now, d'you hear? If you want it to last. Do you see those threads? Well, you grease them well and don't go drying it by the fire, that'll ruin the leather.' The smooth feel in the cup of the hand, the black horseshoe ridges, the gleaming white sitting on newly mown grass, repeat and repeat the cut off the ground, they say Theo English can cut a point from the sideline. That's your hurling.

'Are we anywhere near this godforsaken place?'

Dooley again to Paul. 'This fog has me addled.' Paul smiling kindly as always. If he had his way he'd give everyone a game, subs on and off, all going home saying it was *they* made the vital pass. 'Relax there, Donny, we can't be far.'

'Of course . . . how you arranged this, Paul O'Neill, I'll never know! Under-twelves? Sure half of them don't know their own age! And is that a tin of biscuits you brought there under the seat? Biscuits! They'll say we're getting as bad as the rugby crowd, hah! Tea and biscuits at a hurling match!'

'Ara, it's just a little something, those lads in there now . . . I'd say they don't see too many good-ies.' Paul smiled benignly out the window. Out into the autumn fog. Still playing himself, Paul could magic the ball out of a shemozzle, turn and twist, a genius, but missing the killer touch, that was the word that went around the sideline. 'Will he get rid of it,' they'd say, as he enjoyed wheeling about and mesmerising the opponents. 'Will you do some-thing with it.' Then, after one last swerve, if he tapped it over the bar all was well. They'd cool down. He got that skill from his mother's people. But missing the killer instinct. 'If he'd only use the ball.'

We're here! Our first time travelling to a match on a bus, that's bad enough for the nerves, but now getting out, will you look at the size of 'em. Word travelling back onto the bus. The size of 'em, lads! Brother Timothy welcoming the adults. We were warned to be polite to the boys no matter what they might throw at us, and say hello to Brother Timothy, their coach. Before leaving, Paul had got us together and said, 'Now look lads, this is only a challenge match, don't worry about the result, the lads in there don't get much time for hurling. Do yere best and give them a game. Avoid hard pulling – there'll be only one winner out of that! Some of these lads came up hard!' The boys on my road knew Timmo had been sent off. We hardly knew Timmo he was around so little. My mother would just say, 'It's probably for his good, poor lad.' 'If you're not careful you'll be sent off to the Estuary,' an occasional warning. But we kind of knew it wouldn't happen. Lads like Timmo, who was wild as a goat, it happened to. Robbing, that kind of thing. We only rawked orchards, the Guards would never take you away for that.

They weren't great, we could tell early on, but the swipes they were drawing with the hurleys meant you stayed well back. Their haircuts were tight and they all looked angry. Then Miney O'Toole went down with a belt, no one saw it but there he was, stretched. A bit of blood on his ear. Wait till this gets back. Paul and Donny dousing him with the water.

'Stand back will ye,' Donny like a wasp. 'Give him some air.' Brother Timothy swinging in to the action and carrying off one of the biggest of them by the scruff of the neck. 'One thing I asked ye to do, one thing!' he was shouting demented at his charge as he turned back to the knot of people around O'Toole. 'He's all right . . . he'll be all right?' 'Ah, don't worry Brother,' Paul came back at him. 'A splash of the holy water will do the trick!' A groggy O'Toole was lifted to his feet. No hope of him playing on. But the game resumed, subdued. They seemed to be letting us get the ball, watching the sideline where Brother Timothy, arms tightly folded, glowered in, but then towards the end they got going again and swept in two goals to seal their win. No great cheers.

The bus chugged out from the grey building into the foggy evening. 'An *industrial school* if you don't mind! There's one for ye!' Donny was relaxed now that we were on the way home. Miney O'Toole not too bad, able to talk a bit. What happened? He remembers the ball going up the field, nothing after that. 'Wouldn't ye like to be sent in there, hah! Ye'd be out weedin' parsnips instead of thrown there at home with yeer comics. Was there any sign of Timmo? I forgot to ask the Brother, with all the fuss.'

'They'd be afraid he'd try to come home with us,'

said Paul. 'The poor devil must be missing his mother.' This was for Donny's ears only.

Why, why is Timmo in there? *Can you hear us now, of course not, hear a child's voice in all the noise?*

'He's in there because he has to be, that's the holy all of it. He's better off in there.' Donny was quite clear on that.

'Look at my leg after 'em.' A voice at the back of the bus, Coughlan.

'Whatever kind of a dream I had,' says Timmo, 'it came back to me and I half awake but I was kind of swimmin' standing up! Moving my hands like you'd be walkin' only I was in this current being swept down around the bend.'

'The power of whiskey!' says J.D. 'Amn't I the lucky man to be off it. So go back to the story Timmo.' J.D.'s eyes were watering with mirth as he got Timmo to recount the events of the night before. One more time. Timmo was still shivering every now and then as he sat huddled near the range of red coals, a rag of a blanket around him. The hat was over the fire. As always, he was able to laugh. 'I was . . .' J.D. and himself burst into another fit of laughing, 'I was on my way home, don't ask me what time it was, sure now being Christmas Eve it can't have been too late with the crowd headin' down to midnight Mass.' 'You should have

been with 'em', says J.D., 'if it wasn't for your bol-
loxin', was two years ago', looking across at me to
remind, 'when the bauld Timmo had to start up
singing down the back of the church!'

'I was only helpin' out the choir. Sure I couldn't
resist "Silent Night", that was my big piece below
in the Estuary. Auld Brother Timser – maybe
because we shared a name! – used to say he'd have
to send me out with something. He knew my
mother, God be good to her, was a good singer.
Am I right there, J.D.?'

'A right good singer. Go back to your story.'

'Where was I? I don't know what time I left the
Foxhound but I had my few whiskeys . . .'

'Listen to him. A few!' J.D. and myself enjoyed
that.

'And anyway, I was fine till I was crossin' the
bridge and the rain pissin' out of the heavens. I'd
say 'twas goin' all day. And the bloody timber of
course was as slippy as, as that bar of soap there,
and then the railing must have went because the
next thing I knew sure I was sailing down with the
flood!'

'Down the Swanee!'

'Easy for ye laugh but I'm here to tell the tale . . .'

'He came out below at the turn where the bank
slopes in . . .'

'Out at the turn where the bank slopes in. The
briars tearing at me and I soaked to the skin. I tell

ye I wasn't long soberin' up!' Pulling the blanket in around him, 'Anyway, the whiskey must have saved me for I landed here at the door . . .'

'I heard this rattling at the latch, and I fine and snug in my bed, when this figure appears at the door. "What in God's name happened *you*?" says I.'

' "Let me in," says I. "I'm lucky to be alive." And I made straight over here to the fire. Perished to the marra I was! What's this you said, J.D.? "You're like a drownded rat!" '

'The shirt, tell him about the shirt! Wait for this!'

'My waistcoat, I still had that on, but the shirt – my fine shirt was gone! Sitting there by the fire, says I to J.D., "My shirt, where's my shirt? It's gone." Can you figure that out?' A great scairt of a laugh. 'Now there's one for ye!'

'And the hat!'

'I still have the hat. Look at it there over the fire, my fine hat! It stuck to my head. "We're together so long," I s'pose it said. Drying out for another day. I don't know, lads, how I'm alive, what! And then the dream as I slept on the chair, like I was walkin' along in the flood, coming at my ease to this shore, just walkin' along . . . What was all that I don' know?'

As I was slowly passing
An orphans' home one day

Alone a boy was standing
And this I heard him say:
I'm nobody's child . . .

'Bad enough to be in an orphanage but to be blind on top of it! She's off again. Is that the only song she knows . . . ?'

'A pity she wouldn't learn a decent song instead of those auld come-all-yees.'

'But a great worker, mind, scrubbing floors in this house and that house, all she learned above in the Home of course. Scrubbing.'

'Having to give up the child must have been a bit of a wrench for her. A gas woman. But fond of the drop.'

'Too fond, and was fond of you-know-what, I'd say, in her day!' The leery eyes.

The two at the chess take pause. Amid the talk and the singing they eyed up their pieces on the board, how to outwit old Bill. The Saturday afternoon game of chess under the high window and as that last corrosive comment filtered through he winked across. 'Charity,' says our normally taciturn Bill, our chess player supreme, 'is in fearful short supply.' He moved the queen.

I hear there was great ructions down at Ted-the-Harness's when poor auld Paul and Donny had to deliver Miney back. Livid, it seems. Any teeth

gone? Looked into his eyes. Roll this way, now that
way. Ted better than any doctor of course. He read
'em it seems. Poor Paul trying to explain that, look,
it was his idea not Donny's but it was into poor
auld Donny he stuck. 'You of all people should
know not to be taking 'em into that bear pit.
They're half savage down there. The boat is all that
crowd deserve, give 'em the boat.' Out into the
street it went. You know the Harness when he gets
going. A mighty different Ted-the-Harness you
have then. Oh, there'd be no more sliotars delivered
up to the field, he wouldn't be at their beck and
call, 'And you Donny Dooley, of all people you . . .'
Of course you know what that meant! And Paul
trying to butt in with his, 'Ah listen now, Ted, listen.' Listen how are you . . . when Ted is on a rant.

The young fella? Oh sure he's fine. But he'll be
at home now listening to that, going on and on
about Dooley and he not even to blame! And
everyone will get it over the counter. You won't
want to be in a rush with your leather!

Hinting all the time about that bit of a thing surrounding poor Dooley. About his mother, Mags,
back the years and the various stories. They say
poor Dooley never twigged – or is that the why
that he never darkens the door of a bar, that he
fears the loose talk, half hints. Sure the past is the
past. But Ted will rake through it all again. And

poor Dooley not even to blame. *There's the child's voice again, do you hear? Listen. Nor do I. In this rattling.*

l'Intellectuel Irlandais

He nudged himself out of the blankets, enough to cock an ear to the radio which purred by his bed, Sunday morning lie-in, then dozed back a little, in and out of slumber. The radio came and went and he later wondered which was real, which was dreamt. If he got the chance he would use that playback thing, but the time – that was the catch. Who has time for playback?

The presenter was crooning, perhaps swooning, depending on his changing state of consciousness.
  'Now this morning, listeners, we have two of our foremost artists-cum-thinkers with us on this, the Dual Personality Show. And I am delighted to welcome you both, Rod Fallow, poet and, what shall I say, a character of our times really? If we pitch Kavanagh as the character of Dublin's '50s, shall we say Rod is the defining lyricist of our generation? And with him – *you two* know each other

of course, but we'll get to all that – with him is the renowned Benjamin Regan, writer, thinker, I would almost go so far as to say *agent provocateur*! Or is that going a bit far, Ben? I mean in ideas terms of course, not violent action!

'Eh, please Philomena!' Benjamin's upper lip is tight over his teeth, the radio tuner seems to mimic this deep-thought manifestation. 'I just hope that I can offer a little, ahem, something to the body politic as it were. If my ideas are sometimes provocative then let that be as it may!'

'And *you* Rod, have I sufficiently introduced *you*? Hmm?'

'Indeed, Philomena, I am humble enough to allow myself be described in such terms!'

'Well, listeners, we have taken ourselves out of our more staid setting in Studio Two and have de-camped, as it were, here opposite St Patrick's Cathedral, here on this little street where Rod has fetched up, in this wonderful, simply *wonderful*, old artisan dwelling.'

'So, I'll start with *you* Rod, if that's okay. In read-ing your *wonderful* poetry I often ask myself, Where does he get these ideas? How can he possibly be so original? And what is this I've heard of late, 'in-verse thinking'? Can you give us an insight, Rod? Us non-poets that is!'

There is a contemplative pause. The radio crackles impatiently.

'You see those exposed rafters? Well, I insert my legs in there and hang upside down until the inspiration comes.' This flows into the room in the languid yet sonorous voice which is a prerequisite in reciting poetry. 'Sometimes it may be hours . . .'

'You cannot be serious, Rod! Our listeners will have to just imagine this. As I said earlier – in case some listeners have just switched in – we are here in this *wonderful* little artisan house, in the shadow of St Patrick's Cathedral – and at this hour of day the morning sun is blocked by the imposing steeple – and with me is the renowned poet and thinker Rod Fallow. And you were saying, Rod, I mean *seriously*, that you suspend yourself from those rafters and . . .'

'Yes, when no inspiration is coming then I have no option really but to resort to the Inverse Method. This I learnt . . .' Was that a weary yawn from the radio? '. . . from that great French poet Shagall when I spent penniless days on the Rue Buffon sipping coffee. You know, Philomena . . . in Paris one can be penniless but happy, just watching the sheer *class* of the Parisians as they carry themselves so gracefully, with that certain . . . that certain *je ne sais quoi*!'

'Indeed, Rod. And moving on to the Bloody Sunday poem, Rod, was that written during your Parisian period? The one where you questioned the popular narrative and tried to give us the other side, the British side? Did that come from suspension or was it an immediate inspirational impulse? If I recall, it was printed on the front page of *The Irish Mimes*. And the reaction you got, Rod, did that *hurt* you? It must have . . .'

'Oh, when you try to tell the *truth*, Philomena . . .' A pause, and the radio sighs. '. . . show us Irish that we must really stop complaining and see the Ulsterman's point of view, the true *indomitable* Ulstery – to paraphrase our old friend Yeats– these narrow-minded nationalists needed to see that they did not speak for me . . . that was my motive. It was shortly after that that I moved to Paris.'

'Of course you immediately searched out the Latin Quarter and became well known for your free thinking, your questioning mind. I find that *fascinating*. And your love of French rugby, Rod. Though may I say this, I can't imagine you as the sporty type!'

There is a figurative pause. The radio crackles its irritation.

'Perhaps it was Beckett's ghost which guided me. You know how Sam loved the French rugby, their style, *panache*. I cannot be sure. But oh, that first match in the Stade de France! And as the crowd began, with that gusto, that great French gusto, "La Marseillaise", the goose pimples stood on the back of my neck . . . *Aux armes, citoyens, Formez vos bataillons, Marchons, marchons*! Oh, what country, what country can compare . . . ?'

The radio positively floated about the room before settling again on the locker by the bed.

'But Rod, I see exactly what you *mean* and who can hear those stirring words without wanting to, oh I don't know, go out and . . . Oh! But then, the words, Rod! The words! Even with my school French! When you consider . . . is it not all about *blood* and *honour* and *nationalism* . . . all that stuff that you detest?'

'Ah, Philomena . . .' The dial on the radio assumes a pitying look. 'Philomena . . . it is the French flair, the *élan*, the pride . . . The pride of a great nation.'

'But Rod, if Ireland, let's just say . . . if Ireland and, say, France were playing, would you not feel the same about . . . about our national anthem, *Amhrán na bhFiann*? Does that not stir you also?'

'Oh. Philomena . . . Philomena, please!'

'You see, this is how I do it . . .'

'For our listeners! Rod is now standing on the kitchen table . . . Careful . . .'

'Luckily the ceilings are low in these artisan houses so that I may, *huff, puff,* get my legs, one, *huff,* at a time up there, *puff,* between the joists, there now the other, and then you lower the head like so . . .'

The radio rattles out a *ratta-tat-tat* on the bedside locker.

'Rod is now suspended, oh my God, from the rafters, I cannot believe this!

'I've read somewhere that the old Gallic composers, *puff*, those in southern Gaul as it was, would do something like this, perhaps using the wine-press, *huff*. We cannot be sure, but I feel that I am with them, *puff*, in spirit. Yes, that great *raconteur* and fellow poet Shagall it was who taught me . . .'

'For our listeners, Rod's face is now quite red. Rod, do you really feel this helps your poetry?'

'Then again you two are so *different* in many ways, one the poet-cum-dreamer and you, Benjamin, the incisive analyst. I'll now turn to you, Benjamin, while Rod is engaged in the Inverse Method.

'We cannot let this chat go without mentioning your latest book, Benjamin, *Cruise Missals*! What a wonderfully inventive and clever play with words. Only you could come up with a title like that!'

'Well, Philomena, *ahem*, I suppose it was a little tongue in cheek, summoning up images of pious Irish Mass-goers as they thumbed through their missals. And of course old Cruiser was a bit of a missile in the body politic! What with firing Mary Holland that time from the *Observer*, which was, in retrospect, perhaps a little harsh, but he did what he believed in, that was the thing. In many ways he led us intellectuals into the battlefield of ideas, the necessary dichotomy . . .'

'And you, Rod, have *you* had time to read Benjamin's latest book or are you perhaps too engrossed . . .'

'Indeed, I very much like the feel of this book, the very feel, and I must confess immediately to not having read it – Benjamin will understand perfectly – it is one of those books to be read on a special occasion. At a time, I would say, of mass vulgarity!

'Speaking of which, my mind goes back to 1991 when some of those fellow-travelling Neanderthals (for want of a better word) wanted us to *celebrate* 1916, 'the Spirit of 1916' they called it, for heaven's sake! I am glad to say I stood shoulder to shoulder with Conor on that one. The Cruiser chose the course pretty much of completely ignoring the sorry spectacle, and I am glad to say our main papers did likewise. Celebrate what? I said. Celebrate what? Murder and mayhem?'

'I suppose the Holland Affair, as we might call it, could be construed as, shall we say, allowing nationalist propaganda, a republican agenda, Benjamin, to be vented . . .'

'Yes, and then again the very . . . how shall I put it, encumbrance . . . of history, the various narratives . . . at least Conor put his stamp on events, he was not afraid of being labelled "contrary". Actually that is the excitement of the man, what led me ultimately to write this book. We may not be always at one with him, and yes, the Holland Affair drew some fire from the opposition, but he *challenged* us. I somehow feel he challenges us still . . .'

'And moving on, Benjamin. Under your nom de plume, Bin U, in your earlier years, I see you wrote some interesting material on Yeats and his contribution to the English tradition, and somewhat controversially you state that he *escaped* the Irish language, that he was somehow lucky . . .'

'Of course some of the diehards attacked me over that, somehow implying that I was against the Irish language, whereas . . . all I was saying really was that Yeats might have had a hankering to learn the old tongue, but isn't the world so lucky that he, that he wrote in English? It is after all the vernacular . . . and so my use of the word *escaped* . . .'

'And that bit where you almost thanked the English for invading! Benjamin! Bin U! How provocative was that!'

'Well, again, in context, what I was saying there, Philomena, was not an insult to the Irish, or indeed the indigent, eh sorry, indigenous language . . .' The radio seems to stifle a cackle. '. . . as some have taken it upon themselves to allege, but rather be glad that we have had English, that wonderfully inventive language bestowed on us as it were . . .'

'Though I see one trenchant critic of yours quotes Heaney – an abiding genius in our midst, I think we will all agree – as saying to be without Irish is "to cut oneself off from ways of being at home".

'Well what Seamus means there, I believe, is that a passing knowledge of the language is indeed a delightful thing – and of course you know I have written extensively on Heaney and wish him many more years of creativity. And that indeed is a *delightful* way of putting it: "ways of being at home". Hmm. A true Heaneyism.'

'That tune which Rod is humming? We don't wish to interrupt him but our listeners will have heard it in the background. Benjamin, you probably know it?'

'Though he hates to admit to any influences, Rod is a bit of a Joycean, and that sounds to me like "Shool a Roone", an Irish ditty which old Joyce had a fondness for.' The radio hisses 'Siúil a Rún'. 'I think he may be emerging from the trance . . .'

'So, turning again to you, Rod – and our listeners will be relieved to hear that you are again back with us as it were – you too were a little hurt I believe by the reactions of some to your paean to mealtime, "Let Us Eat". There may be some echoes there of Heaney's "ways of being at home", no?'

'Oh, a tenuous link at most. If I may remind our listeners of the opening lines:

Repas, mahlzeit, comida,
let us gather round,

pronounce these names aloud,
now crossing borders
welcoming ourselves
inside familial surrounds
of *supper, pietanza, maltid* . . .

'Wonderful, Rod, wonderful – and *your* thoughts on this, Benjamin?'

'One of Rod's finest to date. Language after language was invited, shall we say, to a universal meal, "Sit down!" it said. "Sit down and let us linger . . ." And while I take your point that the Irish for "meal" was not perhaps used . . .'

'*Béile*, no? If my school Irish is not even rustier than my French!'

'Indeed, but it must be remembered after all that Rod is a recognised *international* poet geared towards the avant-garde, shall we say, in world literature, the *sine qua non* of which is the teasing out of what possible echoes might reverberate with, shall we say, the reader in Brazil? And the writer is, after all, Irish, representative of the modern and assured Irishness. The Irish who, since Joyce, have taken the English language and quite made it their own. So let's be honest, there is no *real* argument here.'

'You mention Joyce there, and I am reminded of your substantive work on Joyce, Bin U? We cannot sign off without some comment on that and of course your *seminal* essay on "The Dead".'

'If I may interject there, Philomena. I have on many occasions reread "The Dead" and marvel at the inverse nature of Gabriel's decision "to set out on his journey westward"!'

'Indeed, Rod . . . But Philomena, of course, while Joyce himself headed east – and the wonderful inversion referred to there by Rod – to Trieste and Paris, his hero in "The Dead", Gabriel, ends up hankering after the noble west, the unattainable, and the romantic Michael Furey who had "a very good voice" – just like Joyce himself really. Again, there is the dichotomy . . .'

'Yes, well, there listeners, we have to leave it. We could of course go on all day. And so we wind off another edition of the Dual Personality Show and, as I speak, Rod is assuming once again the Inverse Position in the rafters and Benjamin, of all people, is trying to emulate the feat and I leave you with Rod issuing instructions to Benjamin, or Bin U – perhaps you are a fan of both! – who is trying valiantly to follow these instructions as they have come down through the Gallic corridors of history, as relayed to Rod by one Shagall . . .'

The radio brings on a happy tune.

One Christmas Eve

The bundle came over the wall, fell, and was not redeemed. Christmas Eve and scuttered. Let us see. The boat wobbled over the Irish Sea (seeing as we own it) and spewed out its passengers onto the North Wall, the sing song had been good. Connemara men had appreciated 'Peigí Leitir Móir' sufficiently nasal and off key. Brought into their grasp. It had been a good trip, save for the vomit in the jacks which meant quick delivery and out. Bonhomie on the way back to the Emerald Isle. This was the only way to look at Ireland: from a boat, approaching, in the dark.

The bundle came over the wall. Let us see. Ignominy yes, the bundle arose. It's me. Welcome home, gather yourself. Shake your fist at Behan, at Kavanagh, all the drinkers of the realm, inside it, outside it, wanting to be outside it, nevertheless back from London. *I'm back from London*. Make way!

At the door, to knock or not to knock, the

blurred question. Knock, the door opens, you stop from falling in. Just. 'So there you are,' disappointment etched on every feature. Fuck drink, but it's too late. 'Who were you with?' as if it mattered. 'I was with, I met up with . . .' Absolution if the collaborator could be blamed. Always the same. Dishing out hurt like confetti, no, snuff at a wake. No more snuff, no more wakes. Give them a new one, one they can chew on. I will, like . . .

The bundle, oh to hell with it. The trifle, that's a decent change, give them the trifle. The head was ringing, not the bells of Christmas Day, the head was ringing out, over the turkey, the ham, the *leamh* taste of everything, I'm sorry there's no English word for it, you'll have to make do. Regret, too late but regret none the same. That *leamh* taste of hangover food, each bite a bite of regret, there go the bells again, in the head. The trifle with its sherry hint, to cool, to cure. 'No, we're off for a week.' 'So you'll be staying . . . for the week . . . ?' Is this the way? Oh yes it is, oh yes it is. This way you're popular, a gas man, here he is, well I suppose you'll have one. Hold on, a song. A bit of shush there, a song. The only way, I'm telling you, there is no other way. The drift begins, we wade in, are carried on the stench of seaweed, rotting, or is it Guinness drying on his chin. The night is cold but roll on home. The key not out, unpractised. Try the window of the kitchen. Only opens so far, then heave in we must, just a little more, remember the centre of gravity, remember the centre of gravity has to be, well, has to be centred I suppose but too late, the body acting before the mind takes to tumble – luckily the kitchen table – it's how you measure luck – has accepted the torso and other parts before depositing onto the kitchen floor, the whole cargo, if a little splayed. Then the door chinks open. 'So you're there.'

No wonder they go to Mass. No wonder they pray.